PURITY AND DEFILEMENT IN
GULLIVER'S TRAVELS

Also by Charles H. Hinnant

THOMAS HOBBES
THOMAS HOBBES: a Reference Guide

Purity and Defilement in *Gulliver's Travels*

Charles H. Hinnant
Professor of English
University of Missouri

MACMILLAN
PRESS

First published 1987

Published by
THE MACMILLAN PRESS LTD
Houndmills, Basingstoke, Hampshire RG21 2XS
and London
Companies and representatives
throughout the world

Printed in Hong Kong

British Library Cataloguing in Publication Data
Hinnant, Charles H.
Purity and defilement in Gulliver's travels.
1. Swift, Jonathan. Gulliver's travels
I. Title
823'.5   PR3724.G8
ISBN. 0–333–42870–6

For Susan, Katherine and Amanda

Contents

Preface

This book started out as a defence of the way Jonathan Swift pictures the body in *Gulliver's Travels* and ended up as a new mode of thinking about the text as a whole. I began to read Swift's imaginary voyages in terms of their concern with purity and defilement and inevitably found myself dealing with a number of related yet distinct issues that included politics, technology, science and history. What links these issues to the central theme of the book is a perspective that is perhaps best described as anthropological. In so far as such a perspective is justified in relation to *Gulliver's Travels*, it is because the discipline of anthropology itself can be traced back to the early modern travel literature that provided the context and impetus for Swift's masterpiece. Hence it is my hope that this book will not be seen as an attempt to superimpose the vocabulary of a modern field of thought upon a classic text that is clearly alien to it. Rather it is an effort to recover aspects of the text that might be obscured from view in a criticism that is oblivious to the terminology and assumptions of that field.

The starting point of this effort at recovery is the hypothesis that impurity is best understood in *Gulliver's Travels*, not in a contemporary psychological or hygienic sense, but rather in relation to rational norms and categories. In every voyage the impure is what escapes categories or threatens their existence; the unclean is the anomalous, the ambiguous or the monstrous. Not that this should be viewed as a purely theoretical matter. It is a central contention of the book that each of the societies Gulliver visits establishes its own particular standards of purity and defilement. If it is preoccupied with threats to its security, a society formulates rules about purity which mirror these fears. In such rules, what leaves and enters bodily orifices is often made the symbolic focus for anxieties concerning what leaves and enters the body politic.

Considerations of this kind are used to offer an explanation of the different ways purity and impurity are opposed to one another in all four voyages of *Gulliver's Travels*. But in its final form the book tries to do more than seek to shift the angle of incidence from which we observe Swift's abomination of filth and corruption; it also seeks to bring into focus specific issues which arise as a consequence of its special emphasis on purity and defilement. These issues include such considerations as the contrasting models of Oriental despotism projected in the first and third Voyages, the conception of parasitism implied in the Brobdingnagian king's denunciation of man as a race of 'pernicious vermin', and the way in which the Yahoos are related ethnographically to the Houyhnhnms in the fourth Voyage.

In singling out these issues, I do not wish to exclude consideration of the humour that is so important a part of the appeal of *Gulliver's Travels*. Indeed, humour is an inseparable part of our response to what appears strange or anomalous in terms of rational categories. As a comic counterpart of the awe that we experience in the presence of the abnormal, the non-natural or the holy, humour arises from our perception of what seems anomalous or ludicrous in ordinary life. In *Gulliver's Travels*, humour emerges from the structural transformations by which the narrative thwarts our commonly-held expectations about systems of ordering and classification. These transformations are never lost sight of and are constantly being recalled by humorous conceits: by the rumour of Gulliver's liaison with the minister's wife, by the tiny animals that threaten his existence among the Brobdingnagians, by the discomfort which arises from his effort to live in the stables with the horses upon his return to England from Houyhnhnmland. In these and other episodes, humour emerges from the violation of boundaries and categories. The absurdity of these violations does not nullify the serious issues raised in these episodes so much as to render them acceptable to an audience disposed to be entertained as well as enlightened.

Though I have been reading and teaching *Gulliver's Travels* for a number of years, much of the thinking that went into this book depends upon sources that lie well outside the precincts of my own chosen area of expertise. Hence it is particularly incumbent upon me to acknowledge the extent of my intellectual indebtedness. In particular, I would like to express my gratitude to my friend and colleague, the late Robert Somers of the University of Missouri department of history, who provided me with valuable ideas and information about the controversy surrounding Karl Wittfogel's *Oriental Despotism*. Here too I should acknowledge the useful advice of an anonymous reviewer who wrote a report on the manuscript for the University Press of Kentucky and whose comments helped to give the argument a better perspective. Among influences too numerous to mention, I must particularly cite that of Mary Douglas whose *Purity and Danger* was invaluable in assisting me to understand how the idea of purity might be approached in rational terms. Thanks, finally, to John McCormick of the University of Missouri Office of Research for providing financial assistance in defraying the costs of zeroxing, packaging and mailing the manuscript of my book.

All citations in the text to *Gulliver's Travels* refer to: Herbert Davis (ed.), *Gulliver's Travels, 1726* in *The Prose Works of Jonathan Swift*, 24 vols (Oxford: Basil Blackwell) IX, 29.

University of Missouri · C. H. H.

*It seems to me that objects in themselves are
neither pure nor impure. I cannot think of any
quality inherent to the subject which could make
them such. Mud appears dirty to us only because
it wounds our vision or some other of our senses.
Of itself, it is not more soiled than gold or
diamonds.*

Montesquieu, *Persian Letters*, Letter 17

1

Introduction

Gulliver's Travels reveals a feature that is characteristic to some extent of much of Swift's writing. This is its preoccupation with images of filth, disease, deformity, decay and defilement. Although Swift's interest in these images has seemed compulsive to many readers of *Gulliver's Travels*, they can be shown to serve a rational end. They are certainly intended to evoke a response that is, in part, affective; their aim is to arouse an aversion to what Swift finds most abhorrent in contemporary life. But they need to be understood not only in the emotional realm but in rational terms as well. No narrowly conceived historical or biographical approach can hope to comprehend them fully. They must be related to the basic structures of his satire in the narrative.

This book is in part an attempt to suggest one way in which Swift's darker concerns can be related to his satire in *Gulliver's Travels*. As such, it is intended to offer an alternative to the classic polarities of Swift criticism. In some accounts, the attention paid to the nauseous and the defiling in Swift's imaginary voyages is seen as an inseparable part of its attack on human pride and depravity, an attack that is best understood historically, in relation to his religious thought.[1] At the other extreme, it is argued that far from representing an assault on human pride, Swift's satire is actually a reflection of his own instinctive fascination with the abnormal, the diseased and the irrational aspects of human nature.[2] In my view the concern with what is impure and defiling in *Gulliver's Travels* is much too specific to be assimilated to broad generic categories like depravity and much too self-consciously rational to be attributed to Swift's own instinctive loathing of the human body. *Gulliver's Travels* does not simply expose, but rather makes use of, Swift's disgust.

The best theoretical approach to impurity as a perspective defined by its rationality, that is, by its relation to rational structures of thought, can be found in the writings of the British anthropologist, Mary Douglas. In an influential study of the relation between purity and defilement, she held that nothing is clean or unclean in itself, that it becomes unclean only in relation to a 'systematic ordering of ideas'. An object, an action or a quality appears impure or anomalous to us only when it fails to fit into the classificatory schemes by which we grasp the natural or social universe as an organized whole.[3]

The significance of this approach is that it suggests a possible hypothesis concerning the relation between rationality and disgust in *Gulliver's Travels*. In the broadest sense this hypothesis argues that Swift's fictional narrative is concerned with exploring the interrelations of the pure and the impure, the systematic and the anomalous. Through the satirist's disgust, certain activities are revealed to be unclean, to depart from the norms of behaviour and etiquette that govern his attack. Any interpretation of *Gulliver's Travels* should seek to come to terms with the polarity which this disgust exploits and enforces, the polarity between Swift's system of values and the impurities which must be repudiated if the integrity of this system is to be preserved.

The polarity between systematic norm and satiric anomaly is matched, in the very language of *Gulliver's Travels*, by another polarity: between the particular norms of social propriety that govern the different cultures of the four voyages and the impurities which threaten these norms. This secondary polarity is made possible by Swift's adoption of the anthropological vocabulary of early travel narratives. Through this vocabulary, he emphasizes both the affinities and the differences between his central satiric norms and the pollution rules of his imaginary worlds. Like modern anthropologists, Swift was fully aware of the relativity of these pollution rules and would undoubtedly have subscribed to Paul Ricouer's observation that 'there is nothing that cannot be pure or impure'.[4] Hence he makes ironic use of this anthropological vocabulary, deliberately exploiting its ambiguities, fluctuations and internal contradictions. Within the framework of his parodic travel narrative, purity has ceased to be a clearly defined ethical norm; it can also become a perversion of that norm.

As we might expect, this hypothesis avoids some of the characteristic features of the psychological approach to *Gulliver's Travels*. For example, it says relatively little about the relation between Swift's preoccupation with the darker side of man and his personal life. F. R. Leavis once attributed what he described as Swift's 'instinct of revulsion' and 'sense of uncleanness' to his personal disappointments.[5] Without denying the importance of the kind of biographical factors implied by Leavis's comment, we can still account for such factors by arguing that a supposedly natural 'sense of uncleanness' is actually being drawn upon to buttress a conventional political argument or to strengthen a rational view of the social order. Rather than disclosing a natural 'instinct of repulsion' that is manifested in the same obsessive way throughout *Gulliver's Travels*, Swift's narrative reveals norms of purity and impurity that are arbitrary, in the sense that they differ from one voyage and society to another. As the norms of these societies change, so their standards of purity and pollution change.[6]

At the same time, this hypothesis also seeks to overcome some of the difficulties that seem to beset the historical approach to *Gulliver's Travels*. In historical criticism, the portrayal of man as a 'lump of deformity and disease' in Swift's voyages is often interpreted as a symbol of original sin and ascribed to Swift's convictions as an Anglican divine. At best this is only a partial explanation, one that assumes a straightforward continuity between fictional narrative and didactic sermon. In addition it overlooks the particular system of values that governs the narrative more comprehensively than a historical approach might suggest is possible. For *Gulliver's Travels* contains its own internal structure of thought, thus providing a context in which we can interpret the narrative as a whole and comprehend its many references to filth and defilement.

Some neglected features of its imaginary societies may also become clear at the same time, in particular the structure of assumptions by which these societies seek to defend themselves against real or imagined enemies. Generally speaking Swift's imaginary worlds are anthropological rather than historical; that is, they draw upon his observations of contemporary characters and events but project these observations onto a geographically or temporally distant context of the primitive and the exotic. Moreover the customs and institutions of these societies have a style and are reducible to systems that provide the conceptual boundaries by which the impure and the anomalous are defined.

I

The general features of Swift's imaginary societies can easily be outlined. In the first place each society is a world unto itself, a self-contained cosmos that is separated by clearly delineated natural boundaries from the larger world beyond. This is obvious enough, but boundaries appear in other contexts besides those of national frontier and geographical region; in particular they are also involved in the artificial contrivances by which town is distinguished from country, the sacred from the profane, etc. It is characteristic of such artificial boundaries in *Gulliver's Travels* that they are a potential source of conflict and anxiety. The most sharply defined boundary is the gulf separating the Flying Island of Laputa from the continent of Balnibarbi below. We recognize that this vertical axis corresponds to the social and intellectual conflicts that are threatening to tear the world of Laputa-Balnibarbi asunder. There is a clear relationship between the hierarchies of speculative and practical science, of nobility and commoners and the division of the world into flying island and land continent. On the other hand, the horizontal boundary dividing the contiguous islands of Lilliput and *Blefescu* is duplicated in the struggle for power of two equally matched factions.

The presence of boundaries in the worlds Gulliver visits is related to another characteristic of these worlds, their articulation into parts. Everything is divided, classified, numbered off into degrees, grades, lengths, weights, etc. This articulation is not presented in *Gulliver's Travels* as an isolated phenomenon, but as part of a total process of ordering in which astronomy, laws, customs and agriculture are organized into a system of relationships. Throughout *Gulliver's Travels*, this process is justified by the assumption of a symmetry between nature and culture: thus the most obvious focus to which a system of relationships is anchored is the natural terrain. For example Lilliput is a tiny island, and its diminutive size contributes to the rational efficiency with which its various parts are organized. Within the island the existing space is divided into 40-foot square enclosures in such a way that the whole appears to Gulliver as a 'continued Garden' and its separate fields like 'so many Beds of Flowers'.[7] The regularity of this pattern, more reminiscent of the gardens of Holland than of France, is paralleled in the internal articulation of elements in '*Mildendo*', the metropolis of Lilliput. The city is an 'exact Square', each side of which is five hundred feet long; this square is in turn subdivided by two intersecting avenues into four quarters. At the centre of the city, the emperor's palace is enclosed by a wall 'two Foot high' and separated by three concentric courts and a distance of twenty feet from the remainder of the buildings (XI,46–7). It is probable that the plan of the city has a significance that extends beyond its rigid geometric design. The emperor who dwells in the centre of the city is also depicted as the centre of the universe, whereas the dwellings on the periphery belong to his subjects, who, since they are excluded from this power and are thus inevitably spectators, constitute the audience for the great spectacles over which he presides.

Every system in which groups are defined and distinguished implies a potential ranking of categories, a principle of classification by subordination. In Lilliput etiquette requires the subject to prostrate himself on the ground before the emperor. Appointments to great offices are chosen by contests involving leaping and crawling or rope dancing. Factions are distinguished by high heels and low heels or big endians and little endians. Such permutations all use the same set of up/down discriminations, but the pattern of the total system varies from community to community. The Houyhnhnm hierarchy is defined in terms of colour, but this society differs from the other societies in *Gulliver's Travels* in the sense that its rankings are natural, not arbitrary. Rather than stemming from the will of the ruler, these rankings owe their origin to the belief that there is a homology between differences in colour and differences in talent and capacity (XI,256). They presuppose these fundamental distinctions and operate within them as their basic social units. Yet it would be an error to ascribe all the virtues of the Houyhnhnm society to its hierarchy based on a stratification ordered by descent.

It is not the only mode of relationship among the Houyhnhnms and if it were, it is doubtful that even these virtuous horses would be expected to avoid the conflicts that beset the other societies of *Gulliver's Travels*. For while gradations of prestige and deference follow this natural pattern quite exactly, it is buttressed by a very different, rational form of political organization. Within the established framework of a vertical ranking pattern, Swift superimposes a horizontal system of representative government. This system produces another web of ties spreading across the culture, a more intangible web than that which holds the ranks together, but one which is strong enough to prevent them from becoming a potential source of conflict.

The foundation of Houyhnhnm government thus rests ultimately on both consent and obedience, reason and nature. In this way, it resembles the other political institutions of *Gulliver's*

Travels, all of which are contractual as well as organic or natural in origin. Lilliput has 'an Ancient Constitution', while the grandfather of the king of the Brobdingnags has recently achieved what is described as 'a general Composition'. The kind of contractual agreement explified in these arrangements is necessary to the well-being of any society, for it is intended to ensure its internal stability. In contrast to this cultural stability, the purely 'natural' condition of any political organization in *Gulliver's Travels* appears to be one of endemic conflict between king, nobility and commoners (XI,138). When the despotic power of the king comes into conflict with the popular will of the commoners, as it does in Laputa-Balnibarbi, the result is likely to be a violent clash in which one of the two parties must give way. The only natural community in *Gulliver's Travels* is composed of the noble Houyhnhnms, but even this community is socially organized. It seems clear that its tightly-knit structure is meant to be opposed by Swift to the 'herds' of the Yahoos. Where the latter are driven by a despotic leader who is 'more deformed and mischievous than the rest', the former are governed by the Grand Assembly that Gulliver describes as a 'Representative Council of the whole Nation' (XI,270).

It should not be surprising that the anomalous or impure emerges whenever the kind of gulf separating the Houyhnhnms and Yahoos appears at the heart of political and cultural experience. The source of this gulf is the fact that while the Yahoos can be classified as a group or population, they resist classification by subordination. Thus they do not belong to a natural hierarchy but rather exist as a group that is antithetical to the very principle of hierarchy. The gap dividing the Yahoos from the Houyhnhnms is wide enough for this opposition between rational order and natural anarchy to stand out quite clearly. Yet it is also narrow enough to be a troublesome one. The human sense of defilement appears at precisely that juncture when higher and lower levels are sufficiently distinct for them to be clearly contrasted (i.e. perfection vs. depravity), while still appearing to be inseparable (i.e. equally natural). A similar sense of impurity emerges whenever human conduct becomes the object of scrutiny and interrogation while not being regarded as fully human. We can find an example of this sense of impurity in the Houyhnhnm master's indictment of the 'Words' Gulliver uses to describe the 'Art of War' as 'abominable', which is linked to his perception of Europeans as inferior Yahoos (XI,248). The particular domain of the impure lies in this border zone where human actions appear beyond rational comprehension and where their true significance, unsuspected by those who initiate them, is only exposed when it is shown to exist in a region that lies outside the categories of human culture.

The contrast between order and disorder, purity and impurity exists in a different form, as this study will try to show, within every world that Gulliver visits. But Swift also introduces another opposition in the last chapter. This opposition affirms a sharp distinction between exotic cultures and the imperialistic states of Europe. Swift clearly recognizes that this opposition may be so wide as to make cultural understanding impossible. From the ethnocentric perspective of European nations, these exotic worlds are all anomalous and hence legitimate objects for conquest and subjugation. But one of the purposes of Swift's satire is to deny the validity of this perspective. Hence it implies that while societies do constitute distinct kinds, they all belong to the same general class. Comparisons are always possible because of the resemblances they have among themselves, because of the underlying similarity of their social structures. Nevertheless, the variable potentiality for corruption presented by the 'degenerate Nature of Man' also suggests that even if underlying structures are alike, fundamental contrasts between societies are also possible. To compare and contrast two or more societies, it is sufficient to determine their coordinates on a graph of progress or degeneration, superiority or inferiority. The Lilliputians and Laputans are at the lower margin of this graph of degeneration whose upper margin is represented by the Brobdingnagians. The link between these exotic cultures and the nation states of Europe is supplied by the character of Gulliver. His narrative gradually draws the reader from the apparent strangeness of the exotic into something more familiar, into a world whose values are closer to those of his own. In the first Voyage, for example, it is Gulliver's initial fascination and subsequent disillusion with the rituals of Lilliputian politics that create the parallel between these rituals and those of Western European states. Conversely it is his contempt for the institutions of the Brobdingnags that serves to establish their superiority to English institutions. In the third Voyage Gulliver's admiration for the feudal past exemplified by Lord Munodi's estate and the classical past exemplified in the six heroes who appear before him on the island of the sorcerors serves to define his concern for the degeneracy of modern European culture. In the fourth Voyage, Gulliver tries to historicize the parallel by speculating on the possible kinship between the Yahoos and Europeans. The equine nature of the Houyhnhnms, by contrast, helps to establish the utopian character of their ideal and improbable institutions.

II

These comparisons and contrasts are too intricately related to the ever-shifting position of Gulliver as subjective observer for it to be possible for us to examine them in isolation from the conventions of the narrative in which they are embedded. Generally speaking, Swift appears to combine two distinct sub-genres of the *littérature de voyage* in *Gulliver's Travels*. The first is the familiar 'castaway' narrative exemplified in contemporary accounts of marooned men, mainly Alexander Selkirk and Robinson Crusoe, that were published by William Dampier, Edward Cooke, Woodes Rogers and Daniel Defoe.[8] In these accounts the protagonist is thrown into an unfamiliar world, a world in which he is confronted with terrifying dangers and forced to use all of his energies in a bitter struggle for survival. The second is the kind of exotic voyage literature that we find in numerous accounts of the 'Orient': Sir Thomas Herbert's *Some Years Travels into Divers Parts of Asia and Afrique* (1638), Jean-Baptiste Tavernier's *Travels in India* (1676), Jean Chardin's *Travels in Persia* (1686), and most of the third Voyage of *Gulliver's Travels* belong to this sub-genre. In these exotic voyages the traveller possesses a relative degree of immunity from danger and thus can dedicate himself, as a detached observer, to the task of capturing the prodigious wealth and diversity of the habits, beliefs and customs he has noted. The complex societies described in these exotic travel narratives are much closer to the imaginary worlds of *Gulliver's Travels* than the primitive conditions of the castaway narratives, but they do not surprise the urbane observer – indeed he expects them and records them with a bland detachment, a certain objectivity. Gulliver's role as voyager and witness in *Gulliver's Travels*, like the role of the narrator in exotic voyage literature, acts as a unifying force, authenticating the details and making them seem actual. But Swift alters the exotic narrator's traditional eyewitness role; for in three of the four voyages, Gulliver, like the haunted figures of the castaway narratives, is thrust into abnormal situations where he is attacked, risks his life and is integrated into the world of the other characters instead of remaining an independent observer. Yet because of his position as a stranger, an outsider, an individual whose origins are unknown and who possesses extraordinary characteristics, Gulliver never becomes fully assimilated into these worlds but tends to be isolated as impure, as a focus for the anger, fear and anxieties of their inhabitants.

Given Gulliver's contradictory role as actor and observer, it is hardly surprising that he never fully grasps the significance of what he is attempting to describe in the objective terms of the exotic traveller. A fully reliable interpretation of events appears to be an impossibility; but, fortunately, there is another figure standing behind Gulliver – the satirist who manipulates the ironies and establishes the correspondences upon which the truth of the narrative depends. But Swift's imaginative fusion of two distinct kinds of travel literature does not prevent him from establishing a significant pattern of his own.

Despite all variations in content, this pattern appears in all but the third of the four voyages of *Gulliver's Travels*. In the other voyages we find an action whose six successive phases take their necessary places in a narrative sequence. The first phase begins as the articulation of an 'insatiable' yet nebulous 'Yearning', but this yearning is given a concrete and tangible form in a 'Voyage to the South Sea' (IX, 20), a ship 'bound for *Surat*' (XI, 83), etc. Yet as limited as this objective seems to be, it always seems to lie just beyond Gulliver's grasp. Carried away by desire, he lacks foresight. Wholly absorbed in his mission, he is not capable of anticipating the dangers facing him. Thus when he is confronted with an event that is unforeseen and contingent, he is unable to cope with it. Yet Gulliver's initial failure has at least one beneficial result. Instead of allowing him to concentrate on a narrow goal, it opens up his mind, giving him the broader vision that is necessary to any would-be travel-writer.

Evil is the concrete embodiment of the unforeseen and contingent in *Gulliver's Travels*. The second phase of the narrative is due to an 'accident' of nature (natural evil) or to the perfidy of man (moral evil). This phase is best described as transitional state, and Mary Douglas's writings enable us to describe this state precisely. Drawing upon Arnold Van Gennep's classic study, she writes that 'danger lies in transitional states, simply because transition is neither one state nor the next, it is indefinable'.[9] As Gulliver crosses the ambiguous boundary zone marking the transition from one world to another, he is compelled to adapt to new circumstances. The intellectual power required to survive in a natural world is awakened; Gulliver is separated from his fellow men and forced to undertake temporary enterprises and expediencies. All this may take only a short time; the first real change does not occur until after Gulliver completes the transition from a familiar social world to a new and unfamiliar one.

The third phase, Gulliver's initial encounter with the representatives of a new society, requires a much more complex process of adaptation. During this phase Gulliver not only begins to learn the language and customs of a new culture; he also attempts to accommodate himself to a society in which he is perceived as an alien and thus unclean being. Gulliver's ambiguous and dangerous status as a stranger is reflected in the fact that his relationships in this phase are mainly with individuals and families. It is only gradually that Gulliver and the people he is struggling to understand begin to recognize their kinship with one another. The fourth phase is the happiest one in each of the voyages; it represents the period of Gulliver's power and influence in an alien world. During this phase Gulliver attains a much greater degree of prominence than he had in England; he conquers the Blefescudian navy, converses with the Brobdingnagian king, visits Lord Munodi's estate and becomes the focal point of debate in the Houyhnhnm grand assembly. Unhappily this phase doesn't last. Gulliver's marginal position places him in danger or makes him seem dangerous to others. Thus once again, an unforeseen event occurs and the fifth phase, a second period of painful transition, begins. This is a much more prolonged and difficult period of adaptation and readjustment than the second phase; both cultural worlds seem familiar and clearly-defined in contrast to this ambiguous intermediate state. In fact it is largely because of this intermediate phase of transition that the sixth and last phase not only marks Gulliver's return to the civilized world but his loss of vital contact with the exotic society he has just left. In the first voyage Gulliver's growing detachment from the world of Lilliput can be seen in his readiness to sell the sheep that are the only visible tokens of his stay there. While he can remember with precision what he has observed of the world from which he has returned, a gulf separates him from that world. This gulf can partly be attributed to the disillusionment that he experiences at the end of the fourth phase of each voyage: a disillusionment with princes and ministers, with the Brobdingnagian king and culture, with the Struldbruggs, or with the decision of the Houyhnhnms to expel him from their country. This disillusionment contributes to Gulliver's relative detachment at the end of each voyage, enabling him to view the customs and institutions of the societies he has encountered with dispassion. In a way it also contributes to the satiric mood, since it removes the observer from the thing observed. Ironically Gulliver's disillusionment also leads to the revival of his 'insatiable Desire of seeing foreign Countries' (XI, 80). It is only when Gulliver is freed from the trammels of one adventure that he is able to undertake another. At the end of the fourth Voyage, where Gulliver is unable to efface his memories of the Houyhnhnms, he resolves to travel no more.

From this perspective the final phase of each voyage is simply the inevitable consequence of those which came before. It establishes the foundation for the rebirth of desire that initiates Gulliver's next adventure and it represents the culmination of the experiences he has undergone in the the preceding phases. The typical development of the narrative follows a progress of human adaptation – the gradual rediscovery and utilization by Gulliver of the practical knowledge and skills that are necessary for survival and return to civilization.

The starting point of this process of adaptation can be seen at the beginning of every voyage, where Gulliver is presented as a man of 'active and restless' disposition, one who is quick to accept the opportunity of a voyage, but is unable to anticipate emergencies or truly control a ship or its crew. Not that he does not possess a thorough knowledge of the art of navigation, but he never makes use of this knowledge, never makes a decision or effectively deals with the crisis confronting him. In the first Voyage, Gulliver's failure to 'get Business among the Sailors' in England (XI, 20) is matched by his failure to 'discover any Sign of Houses or Inhabitants' after he is stranded on the island of Lilliput (XI, 21). Initially Gulliver is always helpless, at the mercy of forces that are out of his control: 'I swam as Fortune directed me', he observes early in the first Voyage, 'and was pushed forward by Wind and Tide'.[10] In the second Voyage it is Gulliver's 'curiosity' that leads him to volunteer to go on shore with a group of sailors sent in search of fresh water, and it is curiosity that prompts him to leave the others. Gulliver's subsequent lament underlines his 'Folly and Wilfulness' not only in undertaking the voyage against the advice of others, but also in allowing himself to be marooned. In the third voyage, Gulliver's 'Thirst of seeing the World' is repaid by yet another storm and by the pirates who set him adrift in the canoe. Though Gulliver discovers an island and gathers eggs in an effort to survive, he is unable to dispel the 'Disquiets' that afflict his 'mind'. The last voyage is marked by an even worse disaster. Having failed to learn the lesson of the earlier voyages, Gulliver is unable to discern the 'Buccaneers' among the sailors he has recruited after his initial crew has been stricken by illness and pays for his obtuseness by the mutiny which leads to his being set ashore against his will.

By the end of each voyage, however, Gulliver is presented as quite a different kind of mariner and explorer. It is Gulliver's prudence that leads him to open up his box and call for help after it has been dropped into the sea by the eagle near the conclusion of the second Voyage. In his encounter with the Dutch sailors Gulliver displays courage in refusing to 'trample on the Crucifix' and resourcefulness in parrying their questions. In the last voyage, Gulliver is able to navigate his canoe successfuly enough to discover the island where he is eventually rescued by the Portuguese sailors. But the most evident demonstration of his mastery is his discovery of the boat that enables him to escape from Lilliput. As the prelude to a longer voyage, Gulliver subsequently presides over the outfitting of this vessel with two sails by five hundred Blefescuans.

Gulliver's activity as a shipwright thus reveals another aspect of his practical skills as a navigator. Just as his earlier plight can be traced to his failures at navigation on sea and survival on land, it is also clear that his subsequent successes are more complex than we might have imagined, extending not merely to seamanship but also to carpentry and other manual skills. In the first Voyage, Gulliver not only directs the outfitting of his boat but also makes his own table and chair. A similar resourcefulness makes itself apparent in the second Voyage, where Gulliver supervises the construction of his box and of the comb he gives to the queen. It is true that there is nothing comparable to these activities in the third Voyage, but in the last narrative, Gulliver shows an even greater variety of skills, baking his own bread and clothes, fashioning two chairs and making the Indian canoe with the assistance of the sorrel nag. Gulliver certainly possesses all these skills from the very start, but it is only in the context of his adaptation to an alien world that he acquires the poise and resourcefulness to put them to effective use.

Of course it would be wrong to expect to discover in *Gulliver's Travels* the kind of psychological consistency we find in the novel. What we are looking for is a structure, a pattern, a dominant contrast between the beginning and the ending of each voyage. The basic pattern that *Gulliver's Travels* enacts is just what its protagonists' initial wilfulness foretells. Throughout the four voyages Gulliver's transition from a familiar to an alien world is characterized by misfortune and incompetence – the direct result of his folly and restlessness. Conversely his return to civilization is marked by good fortune and resourcefulness – the outcome of the newly-won insight he has gained during his adventures. This insight takes different forms during the four voyages – it is most evident in the knowledge he gains of ministers and princes in Lilliput and in his discovery of his affinity with the Yahoos in Houyhnhnmland. But it can also be found in his growing awareness of his creaturely limitations in the kingdom of the Brobding-nags and in his disillusionment with the Struldbruggs at the end of the third Voyage. In each instance Gulliver's inner insight is accompanied by an efflorescence of the external skills that had been conspicuously missing at the beginning of his voyage.

This pattern is most fully evident in the fourth Voyage. After Gulliver has settled down to live with the Houyhnhnms, he enjoys 'perfect Health of Body, and Tranquility of Mind' as he busies himself weaving, building and plastering. Appropriately enough, these simple manual activities do not entail the corruptions Gul-liver associates with European culture:

> I did not feel the Treachery or Inconstancy of a Friend, nor the Injuries of a secret or open Enemy. I had no Occasion of bribing, flattering or pimping, to procure the Favour of any great Man, or of his Minion. I wanted no Fence against Fraud or Oppression: Here was neither Physician to destroy my Body, nor Lawyer to ruin my Fortune: No Informer to watch my Words and Actions, or forge Accusations against me for Hire: Here were no Gibers, Censurers. . . . No Lords, Fidlers, Judges or Dancing-masters. (XI, 276–7)

Gulliver's manual labour, then, is less an extension of European culture than an alternative to it – his technical expertise emerges as the material counterpart of his health and tranquility. To be sure his happiness is short-lived, but his proficiency as a craftsman suggests that the response evoked by Swift's hero is a good deal more complicated than is sometimes supposed. Gulliver is not merely a passive sufferer and unreliable narrator, the victim of Swift's irony, but he is also a man of resourcefulness and invention.[11] He may be the victim of his anomalous and insecure status in three of the four voyages, but he also becomes skilled at adaptation and survival. Even the succession of phases through which he passes in the four voyages emphasizes his transition from impotence to adaptability – from the confusion in which he is initially lost to the perspicacity with which he survives and endures.

These reversals of vulnerability and resilience are central to Swift's satiric aims in *Gulliver's Travels*, for they correspond in practical terms to the double and divergent orientation he asigns to his central character. In order to function both as ironic dupe and satiric commentator, Gulliver must possess the negative and positive qualities which are suitable to these conflicting roles. If this means that, in moral terms, he must be both gullible and prudent, it also means that he must be both incompetent and skilful in practical matters.

III

The division of qualities into positive and negative is not limited in *Gulliver's Travels* to practical matters. Its consequences reach into all areas of social life in the four voyages. Related to the division between the skilful and the incompetent is the division between the pure and the impure, the rationale that elevates the Houyhnhnms, morally as well as intellectually, above the Yahoos, the justification for the superiority of their customs and institutions, and, not the least, the gulf that separates natural perfection from natural depravity.

The idea of purity takes many forms in *Gulliver's Travels*, but in the fourth Voyage it is related to one dominant value, the virtue of 'cleanliness' or 'decency'. The Yahoos are thought of by the Houy-ssentially as being without decency. They defecate pub-promiscuously, scramble shamelessly for stones and are attracted to nastiness and dirt. Gulliver intrigues the hms precisely because he appears to behave with a measure of cleanliness lacking in the Yahoos. In as much as he wears clothes, walks upright, and has smooth, white skin, he appears to the Houyhnhnms to belong to a special class of his own; in fact, he is told by the Houyhnhnm master that, among his 'acquaintance', Gulliver 'passed for a Prodigy' (XI, 256).

In this way cleanliness is related not only to personal hygiene but also to a code of propriety. This code provides the norm for all social relationships among the Houyhnhnms. The Yahoos are regarded as unclean, not only because of their offensive odour and nasty habits, but because as 'Brute Animals' they fail to conform to this norm. But what about Gulliver, who possesses 'some Rudiments of Reason' and is more than willing to satisfy the demands of the Houyhnhnms concerning his cleanliness? Curiously no such determination ever takes place. Whether Gulliver meets the Houyhnhnm standards of decency or not makes no difference. He is expelled by the Houyhnhnms from their land not because he is unclean but because, as a 'Prodigy', he fails to fit into their taxonomic system and thus comes to be perceived as a threat to their culture. They can contain this threat only by interpreting it as diabolical and by treating Gulliver as a danger to the social order:

> For, they alledged, That because I had some Rudiments of Reason, added to the natural Pravity of those Animals, it was to be feared, I might be able to seduce them into the woody and mountainous Parts of the Country, and bring them in Troops by Night to destroy the *Houyhnhnms* Cattle, as being naturally of the ravenous Kind, and averse from Labour. (XI, 279)

Whether the Houyhnhnms are correct or not, their attitudes show that even the perfection of reason can envisage this sort of hypothesis, based upon an aversion to the strange and the anomalous. The taxonomic significance of the anomalous attains its clearest expression in the role played by dirt, the *sine qua non* of natural and cultural disorder. The peculiarly anarchic value of dirt comes sharply to mind if we compare the cleanliness of the Houyhnhnms with the 'strange Disposition' of the Yahoos to 'nastiness and dirt' (XI, 263). Revulsion from dirt is of course an important part of the sensibility of the Houyhnhnms, but it is a revulsion that is as rational as it is hygienic. For the Yahoos are perceived as being inclined to dirt only in relation to a taxonomic system in which 'there appears to be a natural Love of Cleanliness in all other

Animals' (XI, 263). Within the context of this system, their 'strange Disposition' is thus not so much an animal instinct that is susceptible to observation as an emblem of their status as beings who defy the classifications and norms of the Houyhnhnms.

To recognize the conceptual scheme that lies behind the disgust that the Houyhnhnms display toward the Yahoos is not to transform this disgust into a bland abstraction. The Yahoos are meant to appear thoroughly repellant in their attraction to dirt, but this attraction is defined in terms of its deviation from what is perceived as a universal characteristic of animal life. Moreover Swift's concern with the anarchic implications of dirt is not confined to *Gulliver's Travels*; it can be found, for example, in one of his most familiar poems – 'A Description of the Morning'. The central event of 'A Description of the Morning' is the early-morning efforts of the three servants of lines five to ten clear the dirt that has accumulated through the previous day and night:

> The Slipshod Prentice from his Masters Door,
> Had par'd the Dirt, and Sprinkled round the Floor.
> Now *Moll* had whirl'd her Mop with dext'rous Airs,
> Prepar'd to Scrub the Entry and the Stairs.
> The Youth with Broomy Stumps began to trace
> The Kennel-Edge, where Wheels had worn the Place.[12]

Here dirt can be seen to represent elements that are recognizably out of place and thus, as a threat to order, need to be vigorously brushed away. But this dirt also presages the incipient chaos that threatens order in the city. As the dirt covers the 'Floor', 'Entry', 'Stairs' and road, so the sounds of London pervade the city's air:

> The Smallcoal-Man was heard with Cadence deep,
> 'Till drown'd in Shriller Notes of *Chimney-Sweep*.(LL.11–12)

Lest we assume that this conjuction of dirt and noise is merely fortuitous, it should be noted that Claude Lévi-Strauss has argued in *From Honey to Ashes* that a similar linkage exists in a number of primitive myths.[13] In 'A Description of the Morning', the conjunction of dirt and noise is both a literal figure and an apt symbol of the social disorder pervading the city. It finds its counterpart not only in the 'Duns' which, like particles of dust, collect at the lordship's door, but also in the 'Flock' whom the Turnkey 'returning sees'. Allowed to leave its established place in the scheme of things, this flock has become transformed into a pack of wolves that is as much a threat to the social order as the dirt 'Moll' prepares to scrub. The corollary of this pervasive disorder is the 'watchful' awareness of the bailiff – an awareness which, like the efforts of the servants, is generated by a need to impose an order that cannot be found within the anarchic life of the city itself.

Many of these details are deliberately designed to be parodic, and Roger Savage has ably canvassed the literary origins Swift's urban pastoral.[14] Nevertheless Swift's attitudes toward dirt are deeply rooted in a rational system of values. In *Gulliver's Travels*, dangers less trivial than dirt are to be measured in relation to this system. The Brobdingnagian king expresses his disgust at the corruptions of Gulliver's countrymen by comparing them to 'little odious Vermin'. This is a good example how views of the natural world and its dangers give support to cultural values in *Gulliver's Travels*. No doubt there is a certain universality in our revulsion against what is unclean and dangerous. But, as we hope to show, this revulsion is not an absolute, but a relative phenomenon in Swift's imaginary voyages. It is brought into play by particular situations, and it changes as Gulliver moves from one place and one society to another.

Thus Swift's obsession with vileness cannot be considered without reference to the entire system of values that has been built upon it and around it – a system that entails not only an instinctive abhorrence of what is disgusting, but a framework of values or at least of categories into which the disgusting does not fit. The more obscene that anomaly is taken to be, the clearer the evidence that the norms it violates are deeply valued.

2

The First Voyage: Purity and the Politics of Fear

I

In the first Voyage, Swift's shift in perspective tranforms Gulliver into an inevitable and obvious focus for the fears and anxieties of the Lilliputians. Because of his size, Gulliver is seen by the Lilliputians not only as an obvious danger but also as a potential source of contagion and defilement; indeed he says on two occasions that he owes his life to the Lilliputian fear of the 'Infection' which 'the Stench of his Carcass' might spread (XI, 32, 71). Perhaps the clearest indication that Gulliver is viewed as unclean by the Lilliputians is the abandoned temple in which he is finally ordered to be placed by the emperor. Because this temple had been 'polluted some years before by an unnatural murder', Gulliver tells us that 'according to the Zeal of those People', it was 'looked upon as Profane, and therefore had been applied to common Use, and all the Ornaments and Furniture carried away' (XI, 27).

As the narrative proceeds, Gulliver himself is made aware of his position as a marginal person in Lilliput when he is forced, by an act of natural 'Necessity', to defile the temple even further. Having no other choice but to submit to this imperative, Gulliver takes pains to explain his attempt to resolve his dilemma: 'the best Expedient I could think on, was to creep into my House, which I accordingly did; and shutting the Gate after me, I went as far as the Length of my Chain would suffer; but this was the only Time I was ever guilty of so uncleanly an Action' (XI, 29). By acknowledging his guilt, Gulliver indicates that he recognizes the sacriligeous nature of his conduct. Among the Lilliputians, ethical pollution is measured in physical terms; their prohibition against bodily discharges extends even to structures which, like the temple, are no longer regarded as holy. Accepting this prohibition, Gulliver re-

18

solves henceforth to perform his natural functions as far beyond the precincts of the building as possible:

> From this Time my constant Practice was, as soon as I rose, to perform that Business in open Air, at the full Extent of my Chain; and due Care was taken every Morning before Company came, that the offensive Matter should be carried off in Wheelbarrows, by two Servants appointed for that Purpose. (XI, 29)

Such a practice obviously implies that contamination by one's natural waste renders one unfit for 'Company'. And, by the same reasoning, the 'Servants' who are presumably the lowliest members of Lilliputian society are the only ones fit to undertake the menial task of carrying the 'offensive Matter' away. Lest we assume that this emphasis upon bodily hygiene is merely a reflection of the disparity between Gulliver's size and that of his hosts, we should note that Gulliver is never able to erase the stain caused by this initial act of defilement:

> I would not have dwelt so long upon a Circumstance, that perhaps at first Sight may appear not very momentous; if I had not thought it necessary to justify my Character in Point of Cleanliness in the World; which I am told, some of my Maligners have been pleased, upon this and other Occasions, to call into Question. (XI, 29)

In as much as we are never told of anyone who has accused Gulliver of being unclean, it seems reasonable to surmise that by 'Maligners' he is referring to his enemies in Lilliput.

Gulliver's behaviour in defiling the temple is not an isolated event in the first Voyage, but is an exact analogue of the account of his extinguishing the fire in the emperor's palace. There is no other incident in the first Voyage which defines more sharply the clash between Gulliver's values and those of his hosts. Although heroic and utilitarian from his own eminently practical point of view, he is both defiled and defiling from the perspective of the Lilliputians. What he has done, without knowing it and with no evil intent or criminal violation, is, nonetheless, a desecration. Through a rule that bodily discharges pollute palaces as well as temples, Gulliver thus finds himself once again cut off from Lilliputian society.[1] That his action is as irreparable as the murder which initially dishonoured the temple is indicated by the Empress's order that 'those Buildings should never be repaired for her use' (XI, 56). Although the emperor promises Gulliver a 'Pardon in form', the fact that he is unable or unwilling to procure it only serves to underscore the extent to which Gulliver has unwittingly violated 'the fundamental Laws of the Realm'.

The obvious question to ask about this incident is why Swift should have thought it necessary to stage the confrontation between Gulliver and the Lilliputians in terms of an opposition between purity and defilement? The answer should lead us not to Swift's personal preoccupations but to the central aims of his satire. Rather than taking the pollution rules of the Lilliputians as a simple matter of fact, Swift, like Plato, assumes that the human body provides an apt analogy for the body politic.[2] In a perspective that extends and deepens this analogy, Mary Douglas has shown how the entrances and exits of the human body can be a major source of symbolism for a society and its discontents. Rituals expressing anxieties about the body's orifices have their counterpart in laws and institutions that embody fears about man's anarchic tendencies. In this equation, the rigidity of social boundaries is suggested by the rigidity of the rituals on what enters and what leaves the body. 'The rituals work on the body politic', writes Mary Douglas, 'through the rituals of the human body.'[3]

Seen from this perspective, the first Voyage may be read as an ironic fable of a society riddled by fear, its theme the baleful consequences of this fear on its laws and institutions. This theme is reflected not only in the petty intrigues, jealousies, rivalries and conflicts of the Lilliputians, but also in the inflexibility of their taboos on bodily discharges, taboos that reflect their obsessions concerning the entrance of dangerous impurities into their system. In Swift's satire the model of the human body becomes a doubly appropriate symbolic focus for the anxieties of the Lilliputians concerning a 'violent Faction at home, and the Danger of an Invasion by a most potent Enemy from abroad' (XI, 48). Just as they treat the political body as if it were a beleaguered city, every entrance and exit guarded for spies and traitors, so they treat the human body in a similar manner. In the words of Mary Douglas, 'the threatened boundaries of their body politic' are 'mirrored in their care for the integrity, unity and purity of the physical body.[4]

Once we recognize the role of this analogy in the first Voyage, it

becomes easier to account for the many references to bodily functions that pervade the text and provide a rich lode for biographical
speculation. Gulliver serves in two interrelated ways, being both a
physical anomaly and a political outsider in Lilliput. As a physical
giant, Gulliver is by necessity subject to all the demands of his size.
To satisfy his gargantuan appetite, the emperor is forced to levy a
heavy tax on the physical resources of his subjects: 'an Imperial
Commission was issued out, obliging all the Villages nine hundred
Yards around the City, to deliver in every Morning six Beeves,
forty Sheep, and other Victuals . . . together with a proportionable
Quantity of Bread and Wine, and other Liquors' (XI, 32, 33). On the
other hand, Gulliver is not only a physical prodigy, forced into
isolation by the disparities of his size. He is also a political interloper and thus a potential threat to Lilliputian stability. And by
attempting to adapt himself to Lilliputian customs and institutions,
he exposes the poisonous atmosphere of its 'palace politics', the
reality behind its facade of courtly respectability. In the relationship that Swift thus establishes between these two poles, we can
recognize the parallelism that is the basis of his satire, namely the
link between political fears and pollution rules. Within the context
of their palace politics, the tendency of the Lilliputians to perceive
Gulliver with suspicion and hostility is the same as their proneness
to regard him as a locus of contagion. And, conversely, their
readiness to view his action in putting out the fire in the palace as a
sacrilege is identical with their willingness to regard him as a
traitor.

II

The pollution rules of the Lilliputians are not merely the embodiment of their fears concerning internal and external threats. These
rules are also the vestige of a society that was once truly moral. In
his account of the 'original Institutions' of the Lilliputians, Gulliver
seeks to discover how this society originally sought to preserve
itself from danger. Given the fact that the goal of Lilliputian
statecraft was to preserve the commonweal from its enemies, real
or imagined, how did it initially attain this goal?

The answer, we learn from Gulliver's account, was by taking
steps to preserve the integrity of those who were charged with
carrying on the ordinary business of government. In view of the

pre-eminence given to the emperor of Lilliput, we might expect to
find a form of divine right kingship in which positions of authority
are determined by social rank. Instead we find a society that
reflects the unsettled situation of England in the Age of Walpole.
In this society positions of responsibility are open to competition,
hard to maintain and always liable to corruption by the court.
Rather than affirming the validity of a divinely instituted monarchy, the utopian institutions of the Lilliputians are framed in the
language of what has been called a 'country ideology'.[5] Derived
from older traditions of civic humanism, the country ideology
embodied the view that a balance of power was essential if the
absolutist tendencies of the king and his ministers were to be
checked. From the perspective of this ideology, the underlying
theme of the original Lilliputian institutions is protection – the
protection of the virtue and independence of the government
against the encroachments of the court and king. To this end, they
offer a number of built-in devices that are clearly intended as
safeguards against corruption. The first is the principle of reciprocity between accused persons and their 'Informers'; this is
designed to establish an equilibrium in which neither side of a
dispute is encouraged to take advantage of his position. The
second is a penal system in which fraud is punished much more
severely (i.e. by death) than theft. The third is an arrangement
where 'good Morals' rather than 'great Abilities' are the criteria by
which 'Persons' are chosen for employment. Basic to the success of
the whole system of safeguards are the efforts of the Lilliputians to
demystify the very art of government itself. According to Gulliver,
they

> believe that the common Size of human Understandings, is
> fitted to some Station or other; and that Providence never in-
> tended to make the Management of publick Affairs a Mystery, to
> be comprehended only by a few Persons of sublime Genius, of
> which there seldom are three born in an Age. (XI, 59)

In such a context, power cannot be expected to flow from a
divinely ordained emperor, but only from divinity itself. Hence it
is not surprising that 'the Disbelief of a Divine Providence' is the
one stipulation which 'renders a Man uncapable of holding any
publick Station' (XI, 60).

The other major safeguard against corruption is embodied in the system of 'publick Nurseries' (XI, 61). It was owing to this system that Lilliputian society originally maintained its rationalized yet hierarchical character. Each broad grouping occupies a fixed rank within the social order, a rank apparently determined in some unspecified way by tradition and inheritance. At the same time, it was owing to the 'publick Nurseries' that members within these broad social goups were placed on an equal footing. Instead of depending on their parents for their education, Lilliputians were originally left to be brought up by others. Among the children, this would have had the effect of disrupting the traditional bonds of allegiance upon which any patronage system based on kinship must invariably be based. Thus rather than depending for advancement upon a system of favouritism and corruption, they were to be brought up in an atmosphere in which power was ultimately based on merit and morality. Even 'the young Girls of Quality are educated much like the Males' and are taught to 'despise all personal Ornaments beyond Decency and Cleanliness' (XI, 62). As a result, the entire structure is intended to exhibit just that mixture of dynamism and stasis, individual talent and tradition, which its underlying needs and anxieties require.

It is sometimes supposed that the utopian social arrangements of the Lilliputians are inconsistent with the degenerate forms that provide the main target of Swift's satire.[6] In fact, however idealized they may appear, the original institutions of the Lilliputians enshrine a cardinal principle of the country ideology – the need to prevent a mixed government from degenerating into precisely the kind of despotic state that Lilliput has become. Moreover, the rules which regulated the original Lilliputian institutions correspond in form to the rules governing behaviour in the present-day kingdom. Both are appropriate to a society in which 'great Employments' are open to competition, but where these employments were once distributed on the basis of 'good Morals' they now depend on the 'infamous Practice' of rope dancing and leaping over sticks or crawling under them (XI, 60). What Swift actually shows is how easily social rules can be perverted into forms which, though outwardly rigorous, are only a matter of show. Yet even these forms have a definite pattern. In place of a separation of powers in which a minister owes his primary allegiance to Divine Providence, we now have a form of 'divine right' kingship. Where he was once a public servant obedient to divine will, the minister now owes his primary obligation to the emperor. In its degenerate form, Lilliput has thus become wholly despotic rather than feudal or hierarchical in nature.

The political degeneration of Lilliput is matched by a deterioration in its values, a deterioration that transforms morality into manners. Internal conflicts are never concerned with substantive ethical issues but with delicate questions of decorum, status, and of the right to mobilize particular groups for political ends. In these questions, virtue and purity become dissociated. In place of moral rules that are universal in character but uncertain of application, we find pollution rules that are arbitrary in nature but easy to apply. The offense of Gulliver and the wife of the 'Treasurer' is their willing defilement through the violation of one of these pollution rules. Inasmuch as she is only rumoured to have 'once come privately' to Gulliver's 'Lodging', (XI, 65), it seems probable that her husband's anger is directed at the pollution of forbidden contact rather than her infidelity as such.

The deterioration of morality into manners is a pervasive feature of Lilliputian cultural life, affecting foreign as well as domestic relations. Thus 'the two mighty evils' – of faction and invasion – take place not only concurrently but also in terms of the same kind of disagreement (big-endians, little-endians; high-heels, low-heels). The 'international' politics of between-empire combat are directly superimposed upon, even fused with, the 'domestic' politics of intra-party and intra-sectarian rivalry. They are acted out, not between radically dissimilar *imperia* but rather through a system of values which has spread out uniformly through both empires. Politics may differ in scale between foreign and domestic relations but not in nature. Even trivial disputes are shown to have international implications and any significant change in the balance of power between Lilliput and Blefescu is reflected instantaneously in the most parochial of contexts.

The obsessive preoccupation of the Lilliputian state with manners is apparent in the very fabric of its cultural life. For this preoccupation is directed not only towards despotism and domination, but also towards spectacle and ceremony. This impulse is immediately apparent to Gulliver who, early in the narrative, likens the town to 'the painted Scene of a City in a Theatre' (XI, 29). In this theatrical context, the emperor is the impresario, the ministers and princes his directors, the commoners the supporting cast, and Gulliver a gigantic audience of one. The stupendous wooden machines, mobilizing hundreds and thousands of people, are thus intended to dazzle as well as to dominate. To see how deeply this theatrical conception of government has become entrenched in Lilliputian culture, we need only to look at the basic opposition that governs its political system: the opposition between on-stage ceremony and back-stage intrigue. Supreme political power thus comes to be viewed – very much in the manner of a stage play – as a capacity to deploy actors, costumes, scenes and stage-props.[7]

This theatrical model has an obvious bearing on the political rationale of the Lilliputian state. It touches as well, however, on the peculiar character of its standing army. William H. McNeill has described how the discovery of the psychosocial power of military choreography, which we know as army 'drill', transformed European military units in the late seventeenth and early eighteenth century.[8] In the first Voyage the Lilliputians clearly demonstrate the basic rudiments of this military choreography: close-order marching, simultaneous loading and firing (XI, 22) and coordinated maneuvering (XI, 40). Though they lack the weapons necessary to destroy their enemies, the Blefescudians, they clearly possess the virtuosity necessary to dazzle their subjects and impress Gulliver who describes their 'military Discipline' as 'the best I ever beheld': (XI, 40). Their size is also significant in this respect, for it is the very fragility of these toy soldiers that indicates the extent to which their power rests, not on their military technology, but on the precision of their drills and the elegance of their manoeuvres.

The Lilliputian standing army is certainly the most visible element of a society that is governed by an opposition between fore-stage and back-stage, ceremony and conflict. In terms of this opposition, Lilliputian politics can be seen as stretched taut between two contending passions: vanity and fear. On the one hand, there is an intense and highly visible competition for status, titles, awards and prizes. On the other hand, there is the intrinsically divisive character of Lilliputian politics, resting as it does on alliance, intrigue, malice, rumour and scandal. Gulliver's size and anomalous status make him an easy target for the fears that are engendered by this political system. Hence his victory over the Blefescudians virtually ensures his eventual fall from favour. He is admired because of his achievement, but he is also despised and hated because of it, for he is a man apart, an outsider with whom officials like Flimnap and Skyresh Bolgolam would normally have had no relations. In spite of his loyalty, Gulliver is thought to possess the kind of dangerous and uncontrollable power that can only be contained by his disgrace.

This kind of disgrace could only have come about through the internal dynamics of the Lilliputian court; and it is inevitable, therefore, that the agents of Gulliver's downfall are hardly characters in the usual satiric sense. They are not shown in depth or breadth, particularity or complexity; they are allowed no distinctive variations in action or speech; they do not, with the exception of Gulliver, emerge from the political background. For Swift, as F.P. Lock has recently argued, is probably not introducing 'specific allegories and allusions referring to particular events and politicians' into his narrative; he is rather constructing a generalized 'paradigm' or model of a much broader political situation, and for that purpose detailed satiric figures would only be a distracting blemish.[9]

III

Such a model is essentially abstract. Although based on a revisionist, 'Tory' interpretation of pre-eighteenth century English and European history, it subsumes that interpretation to a theory of the relation between absolutism and society. And this is indeed the most striking aspect of the first Voyage. For what it presents is nothing less than an explanation of the rise of absolutism in seventeenth-century England – an explanation in which those familiar stereotypes of current Whig historiography, the English Reformation and Glorious Revolution, have been displaced and in which a new model takes their place.

In modern terms, this model might be defined by its 'semi-Asiatic' quality, since Gulliver describes the 'Fashion' of the Emperor's 'Dress' as 'between the *Asiatick* and the *European*' (XI, 30).[10] As an emblem of his political status, the emperor's costume denotes a historical situation in which the original European (i.e. feudal) institutions of the Lilliputians have given way to the current Asiatic mixture of bureaucratic despotism, palace politics and ceremonial ritual. That Swift has a specific model in mind in this passage is supported by the fact that he describes a similar blend of Asiatic and European institutions in 'An Account of the Court and Empire of Japan' (1728). In this allegory, the 'limited Monarchy' of

Japan is seen as being introduced by 'a detachment from the numerous army' of the Celtic 'Brennus' which

> ravaged a great part of Asia; and, those of them who fixed in Japan, left behind them that kind of military institution, which the northern people, in ensuing ages, carried through most parts of Europe; the generals becoming kings, the great officers a senate of nobles, with a representative from every centenary of private soldiers; and, in the assent of the majority in these two bodies, confirmed by the general, the legislature consisted.[11]

But where the institutions of 'Japan' are European, the current customs of Lilliput are largely Oriental. Perhaps the most striking of these customs is the rule by which Gulliver is obliged to fall upon all fours like an animal, crawl upon the ground and kiss the emperor's foot.[12] The implication is that this mode of submission is as characteristic of Oriental despotism as the Houyhnhnm master's readiness to raise his hoof to Gulliver's mouth in the fourth Voyage (XI, 282) is typical of the European 'Gothick' tradition it has displaced.

The conception of 'Oriental despotism' has become a fundamental category in modern political theory. It is the subject, for example, of Karl Wittfogel's massive study of the so-called 'hydraulic' or irrigation societies of the near and far east.[13] This conception, however, was already a commonplace of voyage and satirical literature of the late seventeenth and early eighteenth centuries. Monstesquieu emphasized the Orientalism of Louis XIV's politics in *The Persian Letters* (1721), where one of the narrators, Usbek, reports that 'people have often heard [the King] say that, of all the governments in the world, that of the Turks, or that of our august sultan would please him best'.[14] The presence of the notion of Oriental despotism in the first Voyage of *Gulliver's Travels* need not be viewed, then, as an anachronism. By emphasizing the Asiatic character of Lilliputian politics, the narrative establishes a definite link between its hard-nosed sceptical interpretation of the English Reformation and post Civil-War eras and the abstract model of society it projects.

In this model the emergence of a semi-Asiatic despotism in Lilliput is attributed to two complementary tendencies, one internal, the other external. The first is an arrangement in which safeguards against the corruption of government ministers by the court have virtually disapeared. Since in Swift's schema the contemporary institutions of Lilliput represent a decline from an idealized feudal past, it was necessary to demonstrate that absolutism replaced a more advanced stage of development; hence the pronounced emphasis on the 'Utopian' character of the nation's 'original Institutions'. According to Swift's account, the central features of Lilliputian despotism – a combination of party faction, standing army, heavy taxation and political theatre – which the emperor used to suppress all opposition to his total power – is an unfortunate consequence of mankind's tendency to enslave itself to idols of its own making. The 'degenerate Nature of Man' is thus presented as the only explanation of a model whose satiric thrust, like that of Swift's other paradigms, points not so much to a better future as to a better past.

A theory of the relation between absolutism and society lies not only behind Swift's portrayal of Lilliputian politics but also behind his marvellously detailed account of its technology. The basic components of this technology are the massive 'Machines fixed on Wheels, for the Carriage of Trees and other great Weights' (XI, 26). Made entirely out of wood, these machines are enormous, highly complicated scaffoldings, requiring the employment of vast teams of government-directed 'Carpenters and Engineers' for their construction and maintenance.[15] Because of the size and visible complexity of these machines, they are obviously subservient to the theatrical aspects of the Liliputian state. Thus while they appear to us like gigantic toys, they are also intended to foster an atmosphere in which the power and grandeur of the emperor are enhanced. In part this may be the reason behind his enthusiastic patronage of 'Mechanicks'; in larger part it is the consequence of a profound change resulting from the centralization of power in the hands of a single individual. Absolutism is the prime impetus of Lilliputian technology, and it is to technology that we must look for the material forms through which the aspirations of that absolutism are expressed.

But Swift is also concerned with a second characteristic of Asiatic despotism. This is an outgrowth of a nation's relation to its neighbours. In Lilliput, the hospitality towards *Blefescu*, which had been a traditional tendency of the government, has become a strictly enforced policy, from which deviation is treason. All the Blefescudians are to be regarded as heretics whose very existence menaces the one true faith and the state which embodies it. They can be subjugated by war or even destroyed by Gulliver's superior force, but all other relations are suspect. The implication of Swift's satire is that it is the emperor's political opportunism, thinly disguised as a religious ideology (big-endians versus little-endians), that actually promotes this policy. Though the Lilliputians speak both languages, the emperor demands after the seizure of the fleet that the ambassadors of *Blefescu* 'deliver their Credentials and make their Speech in the *Lilliputian* tongue' (XI, 55). Thus his desire to reduce the Empire of *Blefescu* to a 'Province' dictates a foreign policy in which ideology overrides more practical considerations and which, as Gulliver observes, ignores 'the great intercourse of Trade and Commerce between Realms . . . the continual Reception of Exiles, which is mutual among them . . . and the Custom in each Empire to send their young Nobility to the other' (XI, 55).

In the first Voyage, then, Swift demytholgizes English history with rigour and clarity; but his intention is to do much more than that; he proposes a new model of absolutism in which politics, technology and religion are seen as interrelated parts of a single whole. This model starts by identifying the hegemony of an imperial court based on patronage and corruption and then proceeds to indicate the dissolution of an older vertical hierarchy into a horizontal network of contending factions, sects and cliques. Because of his double orientation, in that he is both a political leader and priest king, the emperor is at the center of the conjunction of two patterns, the congruity of which Swift is at pains to emphasize. On the one hand, by making use 'of only low Heels in the Administration of his Government' (XI, 48), he perpetuates the intra-party strife that finds its expression in the palace politics of his court. On the other hand, by favouring 'the *Big-Indian* Exiles', he presides over a sectarian conflict which is reflected in the 'bloody War' that has raged between the two empires for forty years. Lilliputian technology also expresses and translates the dual pattern of its absolutism. It does so by combining two functions. The first is military, the transportation of trees and heavy weights. The second is theatrical, the glorification of the emperor's power before his subjects. And the overlapping of these two functions in the colossal machines that so startle and awe Gulliver shows clearly that in Swift's model Asiatic despotism stems from both these patterns.

The first Voyage cogently demonstrates the satiric uses of this absolutist model, since it creates an atmosphere of detachment through the use of ironic contrasts. The diminutive size of the Lilliputians, for example, is incongruously juxtaposed with the monumentalizing impulse of their culture, just as Gulliver's gigantic dimension is contrasted with his servile posture as an adoring subject of the emperor. The pollution rules of the Lilliputians serve a similar function, being either ironic in their rigidity or achieving irony through the conjunction of Lilliputian taboos and the fears they actually mask. Flimnap and Bolgolam may believe that Gulliver's 'Intercourse' with the ambassadors of *Blefescu* is a 'Mark ' of 'Disaffection' but to Gulliver, it is just a result of the 'good Offices' he has charitably performed for them at the Lilliputian court. The main purpose of these contrasts is to illuminate the gulf that lies between ambition and reality, between the grandiose pretensions of the Lilliputians and the secret corruptibility which constantly threatens to betray these pretensions. This is an aspect of Swift's satire that deserves more attention than it has usually received. For the main burden of its attack is political as well as moral. Rather than merely pointing at specific human targets, it seeks to draw attention to the institutional structure. It does not simply expose malice and hypocrisy; it also lashes out at the political system that makes these possible.

No less important as a consequence of this mode of generalized satire is its insistence that human vice and evil are an inseparable feature of Asiatic despotism. Thus, unlike modern students of the subject, Swift bases his model on a conception of human behaviour, a conception that traces despotism to certain 'universal' propensities in man's nature. As a consequence, Swift is never faced with the difficulty confronting modern historians of Oriental despotism, the difficulty of reconciling its stratified bureaucratic organization with inefficiency, decentralization, low-level management, periods of liberalization, etc. All these variations are theoretically possible in a system that by its very nature is riddled with corruption and feeds upon the very basest elements in human nature. Indeed, for Swift absolutism is not really Asiatic in origin, the product of a regional or ethnic culture, but a ubiquitous impulse that appears anywhere in the world, that develops in unforeseen directions, and that subverts alien social systems by exerting its influence in unanticipated and unwelcome ways.

3

The Brobdingnagian King and the Abomination of Creeping Things

I

In the 'mirror reversal' which marks the shift from the first to the second Voyage, we find a similar reversal in attitudes toward purity and defilement. When compared with the Lilliputians, the Brobdingnagians appear to be quite relaxed in their views of hygiene and pollution. Eschewing a strict code of conduct at court, the Brobdingnagian king and queen allow their 'Maids of Honour' considerable latitude in behaviour. And rather than maintaining hospitals for the incarceration of the old and diseased, they are willing to grant their beggars the liberty to roam freely through the streets of Lorbrulgrud, the capital city of the kingdom. The importance of this shift in attitude is vividly illustrated in a different point of view toward architectural design. Far from being conceived of in formal terms the major structures of the Brobdingnagian kingdom appear to have been erected in total disregard of geometric figures: the royal residence is 'no regular Edifice, but an Heap of Buildings about seven Miles around' (XI, 112). Needless to say, this shift in the perspective of Gulliver's hosts is accompanied by an equally dramatic reversal in his own attitude. Where Gulliver was once willing to disregard the pollution rules of the Lilliputians, he now becomes preoccupied with matters of purity and decorum. The sources of his concern are of course his size and 'Fearfulness', but Gulliver's new attitude affords a striking contrast to the point of view of the Brobdingnagian monarch: where Gulliver is preoccupied with surfaces and appearances, the Brobdingnagian prince brings a perspective in which aesthetic and ethical categories are united.

31

In the light of this double reversal in perspective, Gulliver's position in the second book becomes a little clearer, for it is no less anomalous than in the first. The farmer is certainly aware of this fact; his treatment of Gulliver, though exploitative, also represents an effort to domesticate the strange, to transform it from an object of fear and disgust into a 'marvel' or a 'curiosity'. The hypothesis of the three scholars represents a similar attempt at domestication. Baffled by Gulliver's size, they characterize him as a 'strange Creature', one which, though not so large as a '*Splacknuck*', nonetheless resembles a 'human' being 'in every Part of the Body' (XI, 97). This apparent paradox prompts the scholars to decide, in effect, that Gulliver is anomalous with respect to the opposition man versus animal. Because he lacks the capacity for self-preservation, he cannot have been formed, they contend, 'according to the regular Laws of Nature'. They argue that, unlike other animals his size, he lacks speed and the capacity to climb trees or to dig holes in the earth. Hence while Gulliver is 'carnivorous', he does not appear to possess the ability to sustain himself, unless he can be shown to feed on 'Snails and other Insects'. The scholars conclude that since he is not an 'Embrio' or a 'Dwarf', he must be a '*Lusus Naturae*' – a marvel of nature. Swift implies that this explanation is only another version of the 'old evasion of *Occult Causes*'. (XI, 104), supposedly banished by the New Philosophy, yet the scholars' account of Gulliver's status as a creature who fails to conform to Brobdingnagian principles of animal classification is essentially accurate. Subsequent events prove that he is indeed unable to preserve himself in a land of giants and is consequently subject to dangers from which his hosts can find only trifling.

The difficulty which the Brobdingnagians experience in trying to find a place for Gulliver within their general scheme of things is matched by his own abhorrence of certain aspects of their world. But while the response of the Brobdingnags is measured and rational, Gulliver's reaction is visceral, embodied in the nausea he feels at the sight of the Brobdingnagian maids and beggars. This is why it has so often been explained in terms of Swift's own morbid disgust at the human body. For the very instensity of Gulliver's own revulsion at these spectacles seems to offer conclusive proof of Swift's own feelings.

Yet in spite of its intensity, it can be argued that Gulliver's reaction does not express a mindless loathing, but reflects the reversal that has taken place in his perspective. This seems especially evident in the scene in which Gulliver expresses a wish that he never be suffered to see the 'pleasant frolicksome Girl of sixteen' again (XI, 119). For the norms which dictate Gulliver's disgust at the freedoms take by the frolicsome maid correspond to the pollution rules governing the Empress's refusal to have her apartments restored in the first Voyage. In both cases, revulsion is related to indecorum and indecency: Gulliver reveals the same disgust at the willingness of the maids of honour to use him 'without any Manner of Ceremony' (XI, 119) that the Empress displays at his own lack of ceremony in extinguishing the fire in the palace.

The analogy is worth pursuing further, since it helps to see the relation between purity and danger more clearly. The modesty that Gulliver manifests in his contacts with the maids is undoubtedly linked to his fears and terrors in the land of the giants, but, unlike the scruples of the Empress, Gulliver's shyness is not cultural in origin. It rather stems from his size and situation and thus stands in striking contrast to the boldness and casual defiance of social convention that characterized many of his dealings with the Lilliputians. Instead of affirming the pragmatic value of overriding boundaries, it insists upon the strict separation of spheres: male and female, big and little, covered and uncovered. This separation is essential if Gulliver is to survive in a country where he is subject to the predations of all but the most innocuous of creatures. Although the maids pose no threat to him, there is a certain ironic appropriateness about the prohibitions he wished to have enforced. For they seek to accomplish on the cultural plane what Gulliver inevitably fails to achieve on the plane of nature: to construct a shield that will protect him from the threats of intrusion and destruction.

But there is a further complication. If Gulliver's disgust is linked to his reduction in scale in Brobdingnag, it is also connected to the enlargement of objects that were once formerly small. Thus, because of his size, Gulliver is now able to perceive clearly (ie. microscopically) the smallest visible parts of the human body: wens, nipples, pores, bodily hairs, etc. That Gulliver's revulsion at these parts results not from their intrinsic properties but from the place they occupy in a system of oppositions and reversals (small versus large) is suggested by the fact that they are analogous in scale to the tiny animals, the weasels, toads, spiders and rats, with which Gulliver is frequently being compared in the second

Voyage. In this sense they can be seen to arouse two contrasting
yet complementary responses in Gulliver: one is the fear that can
arise from the perception of large objects by one who is small; the
other is the contempt that is sometimes evoked when small things
are examined by someone who is large. Within this framework
they elicit from Gulliver a complex mixture of passions that includes not only fear but also a disgust that is akin to reaction which
tiny, hateful animals frequently seem to arouse in the Brobdingnagians.

This fusion of fear and contempt can of course be ascribed to
subjective causes. But the small/large opposition is paralled in the
second Voyage by two further oppositions: rough/smooth and
near/far. The wens, moles and nipples that so disgust Gulliver are
protuberances on what appears at a distance to be a smooth
surface (XI, 91, 92). As such, they are probably related to a traditional Biblical theme. Chapters 13 and 14 of *Leviticus* locate impurity in leprosy: a disease whose tumours and sores affect the skin,
the essential boundary of biological and psychic individuation.
Swift's chief alteration in this theme is to make the source of the
impure not only disease but also natural irregularities. Or to put it
rather differently, wens, pores and nipples are the physiological
equivalents of the mountains and hills that late seventeenth-
century writers like Charles Cotton and Thomas Burnet portrayed
as protuberances on the earth's surface.[1] Although the relation
between tenor and vehicle is reversed, the theological implications
are identical. Both wens and mountains are topographical disloca-
tions on what was conceived of in a prelapsarian world as a
perfectly smooth exterior surface. What Gulliver's nausea accom-
plishes, in effect, is to transfer the odium that had once been
associated with mountains and valleys back to the moles and pores
of the human body.

This interpretation places Gulliver's disgust at the human body
in a rather different light from that in which we are accustomed to
viewing it. It implies that this disgust acquires significance only
within the framework of a rational structure of values. This does
not mean, of course, that Gulliver's horror cannot be interpreted
genetically. Indeed, there may be something universal in his revulsion at lice and bodily disease. But there is nothing self-evidently
loathsome about the magnification in general of anatomical details. While these were thought in the early eighteenth century to
be the products of the 'microscopic eye', they were usually re-

garded as useless, not disgusting.[2] To be wholly convincing, therefore, any interpretation of *Gulliver's Travels* must at least take into account the possibility that Gulliver's reaction should be seen in the context of a wider system of analogies, reversals and oppositions within the second Voyage.

Thus it is possible that Gulliver's nausea is significant not only as evidence of a certain idea of the human body, but also because of its link to his conversations with the Brobdingnagian king. It is tempting to see in Gulliver's disgust at the physical aspects of the human body a contrast to the equanimity with which he contemplates its destruction in his account of the effects of gunpowder to the king:

> That, the largest Balls thus discharged, would not only destroy Ranks of an Army at once; but batter the strongest Walls to the Ground; sink down Ships with a thousand Men in each, to the Botton of the Sea; and when linked together by a Chain, would cut through Masts and Rigging; divide Hundreds of Bodies in the Middle, and lay all Waste before them. That we often put this Powder into large hollow Balls of Iron, and discharged them by an Engine into some City we were besieging; which would rip up the Pavement, tear the Houses to Pieces, burst and throw Splinters on every Side, dashing out the brains of all who came near. (XI, 134)

Here the schematic and imperfectly visualized language of Gulliver's account reveals the immense distance from which he views this demolition of structures and bodies. By contrast, the 'horrible Spectacle' of the beggars crowding around the sides of the governor's coach appears to be connected to Gulliver's own spectacles: the horrific impact of the one requires the magnifying power of the other. From this perspective the king's reaction to Gulliver's description of the effects of gundpowder reverses – or redresses – its meaning, while the same antitheses of close-up and distance, horror and detachment, govern his response. His 'horror' at the devastation wrought by gunpowder is the consequence, as Gulliver aptly puts it, not only of 'narrow Principles', but also of 'short Views' (XI, 135) – the 'short Views' of one who, because of his commanding height, can envision what the nearsighted Gulliver obviously fails to perceive.

II

Antitheses of close-up and distance, horror and equanimity, inside and outside, help to define the range of Gulliver's responses in the second Voyage. Whether he is expressing revulsion at the Brobdingnagian beggars or equanimity at the levelling of walls and sinking of ships, Gulliver's utterances are still governed by his preference for a purity of surfaces and exteriors. Indeed, Gulliver never gives any priority to ethical rather than aesthetic categories in the second Voyage. Instead he describes social propriety, physical appearance, law, language and political institutions in terms of a system of oppositons in which the outside is preferred to the inside, the smooth to the rough. Thus when Gulliver explains that he would 'hide the Frailties and Deformities' of his 'Political Mother, and place her Virtues and Beauties in the most advantageous Light' (XI, 133), he is resorting to the same system of oppositions by which he chastized the Brobdingnagian maids of honour for their improprieties in dress and behaviour. Similarly, when he describes the prose 'Stile' of the Brobdingnagians as 'clear, masculine, and smooth, but not florid' (XI, 137), he is using a system in which the smooth and the florid are said to stand in polar opposition. Antitheses of this sort allow for Gulliver's preference for a purity of surfaces, and although this passage is relatively free of value judgements (nothing is asserted or implied about the superiority of a 'smooth' over a 'florid' style), it nevertheless invites the same sort of judgement that Gulliver has been making throughout the voyage.

The importance of these and other antitheses attains its clearest expression in Gulliver's discussion of the laws, customs and institutions of the Brobdingnagians. For here the value judgements that lie behind these customs and institutions appear to be based upon a systematic reversal of Gulliver's categories. The preferences of the Brobdingnagians are for the inside over the outside, the simple over the the complex, the irregular over the regular. This system of values might well seem to give priority to what is small (militias) over what is merely large (standing armies), but when the diminutive is joined to other characteristics, the value judgement is reversed. Instead of being an object of approval, the union of what is tiny and what creeps along the ground is a source of opprobrium: symbolically it affirms the nonviability of certain kinds of animals, the non-viability of creatures doomed to a precarious existence in the kingdom of the giants.

This opprobrium is built into the structure of the second Voyage. Kathleen Williams has drawn attention to the large number of insects and small animals which appear during the course of of the narrative.[3] These animals gain added significance by the anomalous position they occupy in the Judaeo-Christian tradition. Among the beings who carried the odium of pollution for the Israelites were creeping and swarming creatures (Leviticus 11.41–4; *Habakkuk.* I.V.14), including the weasel and the mouse (Leviticus. 11.29). Gulliver himself compares the farmer's hesitation in picking him up to the 'Caution of one who endeavours to lay hold on a small dangerous Animal in such a Manner that it shall not be able either to scratch or to bite him; as I my self have sometimes done with a *Weasel* in *England*' (XI, 87). The Jewish abomination of creeping things is based, at least in part, upon their failure to conform to taxonomic principles; any thing which has two legs and two hands yet goes on all fours is unclean. The significance of this prohibition for the situation of Gulliver at the beginning of the second Voyage seems clear. It is only when Gulliver shows the farmer and his wife that he walks upright rather than creeps along the ground that he is able to establish his human identity (XI, 88, 89). The scene can therefore be interpreted like a similar scene in the fourth Voyage: Gulliver's careful and meticulous attempt to avoid being classified as a 'small hateful Animal' by the farmer looks forward to the time when he will seek to avoid being identified by the Houyhnhnm master as a Yahoo. In both instances the opposition of animal to man is not merely analogous to the allegorizing opposition of the passions to reason; it is also an emblem of what is unclassifiable, whether in living between two spheres, or in having the defining features of the members of another species.

The Brobdingnagian king's famous denunciation of man at the end of his long 'Conversation' with Gulliver reveals a revulsion akin to the authors of *Deuteronomy* and *Leviticus.* But in Swift's most important reversal of perspective in the second Voyage, this revulsion is now aimed, not at nasty little creatures, but at 'the Bulk' of Gulliver's 'Natives'. As 'the most pernicious race of little odious vermin', the majority of these natives are, in the king's prophetic perspective, anomalous with respect to all the major categories of Brobdingnagian culture and therefore are an abomination *ab initio*. This classification in turn leads to contradiction. In order to account for man's place in a rational order, the Brobdingnagian king has to introduce a special qualification: 'that Nature ever suffered to crawl upon the Surface of the Earth' (XI, 132). In introducing this qualification, this Brobdingnagian king is simply compressing into a flash of intuition the sort of conclusion that the scholars had earlier reached in their deliberations about Gulliver by more cumbersome procedures. Both kinds of argument are related by their appeals to 'Nature' to the hypothesis of Glumdalclitch's 'little olde Treatise'. The logic of its emphasis upon the 'Weakness of Human Kind' leads Gulliver to dismiss its theses as a series of commonplaces:

> This Writer went through all the usual Topics of *European* Moralists; shewing how diminutive, contemptible, and helpless an Animal was Man in his own Nature; how unable to defend himself from the Inclemencies of the Air, or the Fury of wild Beasts: How much he was excelled by one Creature in Strength, by another in Speed, by a third in Foresight, by a Fourth in Industry. He added, that Nature was degenerated in these latter declining Ages of the World, and could now produce only small abortive Births in Comparison of those in ancient Times. (XI, 137)

Although Gulliver repudiates these arguments as nothing more than 'the Quarrels we raise with Nature', it is precisely as just such a quarrel with nature that the king concludes his denunciation of man. As a contemptible vermin, man does not measure up to any of the other major classes of creatures in the natural order, but falls below them all.

III

The dispute between Gulliver and the Brobdingnagian king is of course about far more than a quarrel with nature. The contradiction between Gulliver's categorical discourse on British institutions and the imperfect, fragmentary reality disclosed by the giant monarch's questions also reveals a disagreement over history. In the broadest sense this disagreement takes its inspiration from the political controversies of the 1720s. A central issue in the controversies, which divided Walpole and the Court Whigs from the

Country opposition, was the historiographical question of England's prosperity or decline. According to the Court Whigs, recent events proved that the present constitutional settlement was the best that could be achieved because it embodied the inestimable virtues of a mixed and balanced government. According to the Country opposition, recent historical events demonstrated exactly the reverse: the balanced constitution, far from being firmly established in England, was actually being undermined by the very powers that were sworn to uphold it.[4]

Gulliver's reasons for eulogizing 'his own dear native Country' in the language of Cicero or Demosthenes directly echo one side of this debate. For Gulliver, 'the Affairs and Events' of the past 'hundred Years' have witnessed the survival and perpetuation of a balance and separation of powers: the executive (the 'Prince'), the legislative (the *'English Parliament'*), and the judicial (the 'Courts of Justice'). Each power corresponds precisely to its own sphere, without any interference or corruption. Not only is there no evidence of the corruption of the legislative power by the executive; but each of the powers is distinguished by the wisdom and probity of its members. Thus the different 'Bodies' are seen as related to one another by ties of mutual interest and seen, for all the intensity of their actual rivalry, as inseparable parts of the larger whole.

Gulliver's discourse is inspired not by divine right theory but by an optimistic interpretation of the same ideology that is embodied in the Brobdingnagian settlement. As H.T. Dickinson has shown, the Court Whigs and Country opposition both believed in a system of government in which sovereignty was shared by King, Lords and Commons, but differed in their interpretation of the workings of this system.[5] In Gulliver's establishment version a society that is based upon popular 'Consent' rather than coercion will be naturally harmonious; justice will be assured through a Polybian balance of powers and through the promotion of the 'public Spirit'. In Gulliver's opinion the interdependence of the Houses of Parliament and the Judiciary reflect this, for it depends upon the classic concept of 'virtue' as the restraint of self-interest and the recognition of the superior claims of the 'public good'.

In denying the optimism of Gulliver's account of English institutions and proposing a truer interpretation of English history, the Brobdingnagian king seeks to bring out the inescapable disparity between private interest and public good in Gulliver's discourse. Thus he singles out a number of professions as evidence of corruption of the public welfare. Although generally related to the institutions Gulliver has described, these professions are not confined to any single part or group in society. They are rather one manifestation of a much broader pattern of corruption that extends downwards as well as upwards and, in a later list, will also include 'Begging, Robbing, Stealing, Cheating, Pimping, Forswearing, Flattering, Suborning, Forging, Gaming, Lying, Fawning, Hectoring, Voting, Scribling, Stargazing, Pysoning, Whoring, Canting, Libelling, Free-thinking, and the like Occupations' (XI,252).

All these activities are characteristic of the 'most pernicious race of little odious Vermin' but the implication is not merely a general one: the performers of these actions are seen to possess the characteristics of vermin, that is to say, they are described as parasites. In one sense, they are akin to the lice whose limbs Gulliver could see 'much better than those of an *European* Louse through a Microscope' (XI,113). But in another and more important sense, they represent an element within the individual and society that resists appeals to the public spirit. In much the same way that vermin are parasites which dwell on the surface of a larger host, so the various groups that the Brobdingnagian king identifies as sources of corruption all exist at the expense of the body politic. Their characteristics as parasites seem less surprising when one realizes that their creeping is related to vice and opposed to virtue, to the upright, to the tall, all of which are characteristic of the Brobdingnagian king and his people.

If the king's denunciation of man as a 'little odious Vermin' is considered from this point of view, it becomes possible to distinguish it from the conception of man as an 'Insect' that he forms after his earlier, preliminary discussions with Gulliver (XI,106,107). In these discussions, the king's analogy is meant to bring out the simple disparity between man's pretensions and his achievements. Indeed, the king's language invokes the same kind of opprobrium that we find directed at the Lilliputians in the first Voyage:

Then turning to his first Minister ... he observed how contemptible a Thing was human Grandeur, which could be mimicked by such diminutive Insects as I: And yet, said he, I dare engage, those Creatures have their Titles and Distinctions of Honour; they contrive little Nests and Burrows, that they call Houses and Cities; they make a figure in Dress and Equipage; they love, they fight, they dispute, they cheat, they betray. (XI,107)

By contrast, the king's use of the phrase contemptible vermin appears to have a more complex aim. The crux of his conception of parasitism is that servile dependency, the basic parasitical relation, has a social basis – that is, it springs from a particular kind of social behaviour and not just from a generalized moral corruption. This behaviour is a perverted form of exchange in which people are naively expected to give up more (the public good) than they actually receive in return (private interest). Thus the king asks of the English House of Commons:

> How it came to pass, the People were so violently bent upon getting into this Assembly, which I allowed to be a great Trouble and Expence, often to the Ruin of their Families, without any Salary or Pension: Because this appeared such an exalted Strain of Virtue and publick Spirit, that his Majesty seemed to doubt it might possibly not be always sincere: And he desired to know, whether such zealous Gentlemen could have any Views of refunding themselves for the Charges and Troubles they were at, by sacrificing the publick Good to the Designs of a weak and vicious Prince in Conjunction with a corrupted Ministry. (XI,129,130)

The king's questions point to the kind of parasitism that occurs when people are expected to sacrifice a great deal more than they actually keep.[6] The king implies that such a sacrifice is so unnatural as to be entirely unfathomable and beyond observation. Its danger lies not in the actual damage done to the members' 'Families', but rather in the introduction of a parasitical relationship of egoistic interest into a political system that had relied for its efficacy upon overcoming the dangers of this model. In the king's reasoning, the fact that the balanced constitution must depend upon the 'publick Spirit' of the subject, as a political necessity, threatens to dissolve the structure to which it owes its very existence. For the parasitical relation is not the relation of simple interest that, in Gulliver's discourse, must be overcome for a mixed government to come into being. It clearly is a category that is susceptible to corruption: the parasite who sacrifices the 'publick Good to the Designs of a weak and vicious Prince' is much more dangerous to the prosperity of the commonweal than the conduct of an individual who acts according to his private self-interest. The king's question thus opens the way for an ironic reversal of Gulliver's categories:

corruption is brought about, not by those who pursue their own self-interest, but by those who pretend to rise above it. The ruin of a nation is caused by people who seem to oppose it, not by those who seek it.

This ironic reversal in the relation between public spirit and private interest is almost a structural element in the conversation between Gulliver and the king, because the narrative moves from Gulliver's lofty defense of English institutions to his craven offer of gunpowder to the king. The shift in Gulliver's attitude is designed to expose the sentiment and hypocrisy Swift finds at the root of professions of public spirit. Gulliver rises to 'exalted Strains' of Ciceronian eloquence when he recalls his 'political Mother', but these strains present a sharp contrast to the Senecan accents of his account of gunpowder. And Gulliver's defense of his mother country actually seems to be based on his own parasitical desire for private advantage. Thus he is easily prevailed upon to tell the truth about England; and it is the secret offer of this lofty patriot that, in the kingdom of Brobdingnag, could have led to the political ruin of the kind of mixed government he ostensibly supports.

The Brobdingnagian king's invocation of 'Vermin' is thus not an incidental or dispensable part of his denunciation of man. It relies on the assumption that parasitism arises out of the disparity between an individual's inclination to attend to his own private interest and his incentive to follow the public good. Why is this condition so abominable to the king? His questions imply that it is offensive because it threatens to engulf the taxonomic boundaries of a culture. In place of a society based on order and degree, it fosters a potentially anarchic situation in which nobles and commoners alike are reduced to a state of parasitical dependency. This becomes readily apparent when the king asks Gulliver of 'gaming':

> Whether mean vicious People, by their Dexterity in that Art, might not arrive at great Riches, and sometimes keep our very Nobles in Dependence, as well as habituate them to vile Companions; wholly take them from the Improvement of their Minds, and force them by the Losses they received, to learn and practice that infamous Dexterity on others. (XI, 131, 132)

To the extent that the nobles who acquire this infamous 'Art' become participants in a spreading chain of mutual dependency and mutual corruption, they exemplify the levelling tendency that lies at the heart of the king's abomination of creeping things.

Understandably, this pessimistic attitude toward parasitism and anarchy strongly affects the general outlook of the Brobdingnagian king. In spite of the fact that he adopts a stance close to that of the Country opposition, he clearly regards certain elements of the ideology of that opposition suspect. Thus although he accepts the doctrine of mixed government and balance of powers, he views both the rhetoric of public spirit that Gulliver has been preaching and his faith in the rule of law with suspicion. For the Brobdingnagian king, both these doctrines are inadequate to withstand the rising tide of corruption and anarchy.

Consequently, in his replies, the Brobdingnagian king also shows traces of an underlying commitment to a Tory 'ideology of order'. He reveals this commitment, for example, in his willingness to attribute the failure of the system Gulliver describes to the absence of an effective system of rewards and punishments. This is the point of his destructive analysis of Gulliver's account of the English courts of law. In a society that relies solely upon exhortations to public spirit as an enforcement of morality, the machinery of retribution is never likely to be very strong or very effective. Lacking this machinery, the defense of a community against the corruption of those who are threatening it is likely to break down. Part of the indignation of the king can be traced to the degeneration of the one body that might prevent the inherent bias of English society toward division and political particularism.

Closely associated with this scepticism concerning the efficacy of the English courts of justice is another attitude also springing from an ideology of order. This is the assumption that the widespread corruption of the political system results in the blurring or erasing of the taxonomic boundaries that mark a well-governed society. Since these boundaries are always defined in terms of decorum, the Brobdingnagian monarch's condemnation of English corruption takes the form of a systematic enumeration of the improprieties of the men who occupy positions of power. Thus the king tells Gulliver:

You have clearly proved that Ignorance, Idleness, and Vice are the proper Ingredients for qualifying a Legislator. That laws are best explained, interpreted, and applied by those whose Interest and Abilities lie in perverting, confounding, and eluding them. I observe among you some Lines of an Institution, which in its Original might have been tolerable; but these half erased, and the rest wholly blurred and blotted by Corruptions. It does not appear from all you have said, how any one Perfection is required towards the Procurement of any one Station among you; much less that Men are ennobled on Account of their Virtue, that Priests are advanced for their Piety or Learning, Soldiers for their Conduct or Valour, Judges for their Integrity, Senators for the Love of their Country, or Counsellors for their Wisdom. (XI,132)

The references to blurring, blotting and half-erasing of lines reveal the taxonomic model that underlies the king's indictment. In this respect it resembles nothing so much as Thomas Rymer's attack upon the tragedies of Beaumont, Fletcher and Shakespeare. What the one condemns in the English theater the other castigates in English public life.

The relationship of the Brobdingnagian political arrangements to this corrupt system can be best described as a systematic reversal of values within the framework of a Tory ideology of order. This does not mean that Swift abandons the Country position. On the contrary, his description of the Brobdingnagian settlement embraces the doctrine of mixed government. But the king's Tory scepticism has important political consequences nonetheless. It implies – perhaps necessitates – a traditional structure of power based on the maintenance of order. Myrrdin Jones views the king's perspective as Harringtonian in inspiration.[7] But while it may be indebted to Harrington for certain of its features, it seems much closer to Machiavelli in essentials. Like Machiavelli, the Brobdingnagian king regards political conflict and political degeneration as endemic to all systems, regardless of their structural features. The main advantage the Brobdingnagians possess over their English counterparts is their natural isolation. Lacking the distractions of an external enemy, they are free to concentrate upon internal issues. The militia provides the most important part in their domestic economy because it enables the Brobdingnagians to establish a government based not only upon consent but also upon coercion. The civil wars occasioned by the conflict between the nobility, people and king were put to an end by the 'Prince's Grandfather in a general Composition; and the Militia then settled with common Consent hath been ever since kept in the strictest duty' (XI,138). In this equation, the militia has been prevented from participating in future conflicts by 'common Consent'. Yet it is also the militia, which depends for its discipline upon a Venetian system of popular consent, that in turn provides the machinery of enforcement missing in Gulliver's England. Lacking an external enemy with which to contend, the militia is free to provide the force necessary to keep the 'general Composition . . . in the strictest Duty'.

It is this combination of coercion and consent that transforms the segmentary politics of the Brobdingnagians into the precarious equilibrium of a mixed government. The role played by the Brobdingnagian king and his grandfather in establishing and maintaining this equilibrium is left deliberately vague, but it appears, in the broadest sense, to conform to Machiavellian and Enlightenment ideals of kingship. In the light of Swift's view that political conflict is more natural than political stability, his ideal monarchs might also be seen to anticipate Rousseau's lawgiver.[8] For Rousseau, the lawgiver is something more than an idealized and virtuous prince. Eschewing the trappings of an absolute monarch, the lawgiver is an 'impostor' who prefers to work behind the scenes if necessary in shaping the people's actions. Nonetheless his intervention is necessary because the state by itself does not possess the capacity to legislate its own stability. Moreover the lawgiver must be an individual, since only an individual can possess the wisdom which the conflicting parties necessarily lack. Swift's kings appear to possess both these attributes. It is through the active but unspecified intervention of the Brobdingnagian king's grandfather that the equilibrium of the kingdom was finally established. And it is only through the wisdom of the present ruler – the wisdom he displays in rejecting Gulliver's offer of gunpowder without consulting his advisers or summoning an assembly – that this equilibrium can be perpetuated.

The danger to this equilibrium posed by the introduction of gunpowder is not only the actual injury to individuals, but the reintroduction of a competitive struggle into a system that had come into being by overcoming this model. The fact that the state is susceptible to a 'disease' in which 'the Nobility' are 'often contending for Power, the People for Liberty, and the King for absolute Dominion' (XI,138) poses a threat to its very existence. For the competitive relation is not always the relation of absolute dominion and servile dependency (coercion without consent) that Gulliver had posited in defending gunpowder. It is clearly an antithesis susceptible to dialectical reversal: in the struggle for power, the abject and the absolute can easily exchange places. Indeed, as we have seen, it is precisely the ascendency of the abject over the absolute in human nature and human society (consent without coercion) that the Brobdingnagian king castigates in his denunciation of mankind as 'the most pernicious race of little odious Vermin'.

IV

In the history of civilization, as recounted by Gulliver, the Brobdingnagian kingdom is the only example of change for the better. Its settlement is obviously intended to be seen as its most remarkable achievement, but Swift is also concerned with the place of this settlement in the larger context of historical change, and one focus of *Gulliver's Travels* is his analysis of why certain cultures change, while others have no history.

Generally speaking, Swift seems to present two interrelated explanations for historical change: the first is geographical accessibility, the second a sense of danger – the conviction that one's nation is being threatened by real or imaginary enemies. Together these tendencies are seen as compelling a higher level of technological adaptiveness in Lilliput, which believes itself to be more challenged by alien pressures than does Brobdingnag.

Yet while these tendencies are broadly valid for all historical societies, they are not, by themselves, sufficiently particular to account for historical change in the nation states of Europe. For the instability which Swift sees as endemic to these states, testifies to a still deeper, more concealed problem. This is the failure of their ruling houses to establish genuinely patrilineal, endogamous, hereditary lines of descent (XI,198). What Gulliver discovers on the island of the sorcerors in the third Voyage are the political implications of this failure. It has undermined the legitimacy of these ruling houses and permitted the emergence of situations in which the mechanism of conflict and change can flourish unchecked. The factors which made these houses weak – exogamy, disease, a capacity for internal corruption – also made their unification difficult to the point of impossible and partitioned the European nobility into sets of factions vying for domination and control. But why have such situations gone unnoticed? The very disparities between historical cause and effect provide an answer. In Swift's sceptical philosophy of history, as Irvin Ehrenpreis has remarked, the 'Springs and Motives of great Enterprizes' can be traced to the most 'contemptible Accidents'.[9] It would be an error to dismiss this view merely as a satirical commonplace, for it presupposes a very important methodological principle: a refusal to accept the ostensible causes which men consciously propose to themselves as substitute for the real, most often unrecognized 'Accidents' which actually shape their conduct. Swift's adherence to this principle enables him to appeal to causes of which men are ignorant and hence to offer a sceptical, revisionist explanation of the corruption which distinguishes their conduct both from the moral principles which supposedly guide it and from the puffery of Whiggish historians. Needless to say the ultimate effect of this disparity is anti-heroic: change is produced not only by great individuals in the Carlylean sense, but also by human beings – 'Bawds, Whores, Pimps, Parasites, and Buffoons' (XI,199) – drawn from the very lowest strata of society.[10]

In view of the volatility introduced into culture by this vision of historical change, it is not surprising that there is virtually no society in *Gulliver's Travels* which is not shown as being susceptible to some extent of giving rise to a higher or lower stage of itself. The ranking of a society on this vertical scale is defined by its relation either to its original institutions or to its basic principles.[11] If the relation is one of harmony, the harmony that exists between the Brobdingnagian settlement and its traditions, a society is stable, men become emancipated from history. If the relation is one of conflict, the conflict that arises between Lilliputian factionalism and its original institutions, then a crisis occurs. The ancient constitution is violated. The result is a chain reaction: the form of the government tries to resolve the conflict. It alters itself until a new and sometimes specious identity emerges (the harmony between Lilliputian despotism and its pollution rules). Although it would be foolish to assume that Swift presents a fully developed dialectic in *Gulliver's Travels*, the dynamic of this process is apparent: either a harmony exists between a state and its fundamental principles, or a conflict. Thus it is clear that existence and essence, corruption and utopia, are absolutely interdependent in Swift's conception of society. What is not so clear is whether any society has reached a level of corruption beyond which it would be incapable of degenerating even further.

Thus we do not know which way the scales of history would tilt if all the evils and goods were piled on their respective balances. But we are given the sense that humanity owes the good fortune it has achieved so far to a whole series of miracles. At no stage is its advance or decline treated in *Gulliver's Travels* as part of a manifest or even hidden Providential design.

Historical change is not a birthright, a potentiality inscribed into the nature of every society. Rather it depends upon reasons which are contingent upon a unique and complex set of circumstances. Thus Swift makes regeneration even more unpredictable and precarious than does Machiavelli; the latter only requires the emergence of a great man, but Swift requires the emergence of at least three factors before regeneration can occur. In Swift's version, before the Brobdingnags could achieve as much as they have, three historical accidents (constellations in no way inscribed into the nature and legitimate expectations of any society) had to occur. First, geographical conditions had to be such as to ensure that the Brobdingnagians were not threatened by any foreign enemy and were thus forced into the Lilliputian–Blefescuan political mould. Second, the Brobdingnagian political institutions, which have the same potentiality for internal conflict and self-destruction as those of the Lilliputians, had nonetheless to yield a mechanism, the militia, which could somehow temper those conflicts, and thirdly, the apparently unique intervention of an enlightened lawgiver or patriot king had to occur at least once. Such a configuration of events seems a far cry from the cyclical sweep of the Machiavellian *retorno*.

V

A brief glance at Swift's philosophy of history has thus not unlocked the riddle of progress or degeneration. If it has offered cogent reasons why the Lilliputians have declined, it cannot fully answer the question of the Brobdingnagian settlement. Rather, a review of the not-clearly-understood relation between history and society calls our attention to the natural – that is, to the structural –

reasons for political stability. Speaking broadly political stability is not merely a reflection of cultural attitudes but also of physical and geographical constraints.

The point is important, for it calls our attention to the fact that the most prominent topographical feature of the Brobdingnagian kingdom is its natural isolation. Protected from the 'North east' by a ridge of volcanic mountains, the land of the Brobdingnags is bounded by oceans on its other sides (XI,111). It is hardly necessary to say that in his account of the giants, Swift devotes no space to the life of the sea. Their country is a peninsula surrounded by the ocean, but there are no harbours. This is not a fortuitous circumstance, for throughout *Gulliver's Travels* Swift associates the sea with strife, division and conquest. By contrast, the land holds at least the possibility of unity and permanence. Unity is the foundation of Swift's ideal societies; and here it has been finally assured, as we have seen, by a combination of consent and coercion. Swift gives particular emphasis to this unity and permanence in his account of the Brobdingnagian traditions and institutions: there are few laws and these must be of less than twenty-two words, the number of letters in the Brobdingnagian alphabet (IX,136). Permanence also appears in the small number of volumes in the Brobdingnagian libraries; and the way in which the Brobdingnagian political 'Composition' has been settled once and for all. And, more humorously, in the 'Art of Government', which the king confines within very *narrow Bounds*; to common Sense and Reason, to Justice and Lenity, to the Speedy Determination of Civil and criminal Causes; with some other obvious Topicks which are not worth considering' (XI,135).

We might ask whether there is any further connection between this land-based culture and its utopian ideals, beyond what is obvious? In answering this question, it will be useful if we once again take note of the bounded, encircled landscape of the Brobdingnags. We might see the values of the Brobdingnagian king as an ethical and political manifestation of these '*narrow Bounds*.' It is probably not a coincidence that Swift uses such epithets as 'narrow,' 'short' and 'confined' to describe the king's sense of limits. For at the beginning of an *An Enquiry into the Behaviour of the Queen's Last Ministry*, he writes of his own situation that 'the Scene and Station I am in have reduced my Thoughts into a narrow Compass'.[12] The consequences of this kind of bounded perspective on the Brobdingnagians is two fold. On the one hand, it acts to restrict the scope of their cultural aspirations. On the other hand, it establishes the minimalist 'little England' that Gulliver, the seafarer and imperialist, finds so repugnant.

The concrete outcome of this limited perspective is not difficult to explain. It is evident not only in the laws and customs of the Brobdingnags, but also in the relatively limited 'Height' of their chief temple, a phenomenom that Gulliver finds particularly difficult to understand (XI,114). It is no less apparent in the limited area that the inhabitants of Lorbrulgrud have alloted for the exercise of their militia; indeed, Gulliver finds it 'impossible . . . to compute their Number, considering the Space of Ground they took up' (XI,138). But this sense of limit is perhaps most strikingly clear in the way in which the Brobdingnagians frame their preference for the practical rather than the theoretical in the arts and sciences. Rather than striving for improvements in agriculture that will open up new expanses of land to cultivation or produce yields of limitless abundance, the king is content to settle for the kind of modest but genuine gains that will 'make two Ears of Corn, or two Blades of Grass to grow upon a Spot of Ground where only one grew before' (XI,135).

What Gulliver condescendingly regards as the king's narrow views and confined education also play a major role in his repudiation of gunpowder. For the technology that Gulliver proffers him is one that continually overcomes confinement, levels barriers, and threatens to destroy social systems by obliterating their boundaries and structure:

> That, the largest Balls thus discharged, would not only Destroy whole Ranks of an Army at once; but batter the strongest Walls to the Ground; sink down Ships with a thousand Men in each, to the Bottom of the Sea; and when linked together by a Chain, would cut through Masts and Rigging; divide Hundreds of Bodies in the Middle, and lay all Waste before them. (XI,134)

The levelling effect of gunpowder is vividly brought home to the king in Gulliver's account of its power to 'batter down the Walls of the strongest Town in his Dominions in a few Hours: or destroy the whole Metropolis, if ever it should pretend to dispute his absolute Commands' (XI,134). Here the example points to the same kind of domination that the king of Laputa tries to achieve through the operation of the Flying Island in the third Voyage. But the king of

Brobdingnag, instead of seizing this opportunity, indicates, in his allusion to 'some evil Genius, enemy of Mankind', that he views it as a satanic temptation to presumption, vain glory, absolute power and the cavalier disregard of limits. This does not mean that the king renounces the use of force in favour of farming. Coercion is necessary, as we have seen, in a post-lapsarian world, but in the bounded domain of the Brobdingnags, the militia is the bridge between warfare and agriculture.

Gulliver's offer of gunpowder to the King has often been contrasted to his refusal to accede to the demand of the Lilliputian emperor, that he destroy the Blefescuan navy. The satire works here not only as a symmetrical inversion of the first Voyage, but as a fulfillment of the Brobdingnagian king's prophetic denunciation of European man. For, in offering the secret of gunpowder to the king, Gulliver has, in effect, become the living embodiment of the little odious vermin the king has just denounced. Like these human parasites, Gulliver has demonstrated his willingness to sacrifice his integrity in order to 'ingratiate' himself 'farther into his Majesty's Favour'. Unlike his European counterparts, however, Gulliver fails to achieve his sycophantic aims. Far from enhancing his reputation with the king, Gulliver remains as isolated as he was before.

Gulliver's subsequent 'Impulse' to 'recover his Liberty' can probably be traced to this failure. The 'Resentments' that Gulliver refuses to 'discover' because they 'were always turned to ridicule' (XI,133) reappear – in disguised form – in Gulliver's new-found desire to escape from the confining world of the Brobdingnags (XI,139). Appropriately enough, this desire is embodied not in living things which crawl on the ground but in their taxonomic opposites – those which fly in the air. Gulliver's attraction to the latter corresponds exactly to his horror at 'leaving a Posterity to be kept in Cages like Canary Birds' (XI,139). The narrative itself draws attention to this analogy, for it is only through the intervention of a bird from the heights that Gulliver is able to escape from this kingdom of mountains and oceans. This is the eagle, a bird of prey that swoops down on Gulliver's 'Travelling Box', seizing it by its ring, carrying it into the clouds and sky with an intent to 'let it fall on a Rock' like a Tortoise in a Shell', and then pluck out Gulliver's body and 'devour it' (XI,141). The eagle's seizure of Gulliver can of course be taken as purely anecdotal, one more instance of Gulliver's physical 'weakness' in the second Voyage. But this would be to overlook not only the opposition between the soaring eagle and the tame canary (the eagle and the canary being at the top and the botttom of the mythical hierarchy of birds) but also two significant features of this majestic sky-bird, its flights and predatory nature. It is the conjunction of these two features that makes the eagle into a natural emblem of the kind of prince that the Brobdingnagian king has resolutely refused to become.

4

The System at War with Itself: the Quest for Purity in the Third Voyage

I

It is on the flying island of Laputa that the quest for purity takes its most extreme and radical form in *Gulliver's Travels*. Here inwardness is associated with theoretical speculation, which is given an ironically privileged position over practical geometry. As a consequence the boundaries and categories that serve to define the idea of purity in every culture now become emptied of content, as forms themselves become the object of veneration. The source for this devotion has often been described as 'scientific', but since it is clear that by 'science' Swift is referring to the entire intellectual matrix of Laputan society, Gulliver is allowed to observe its workings in institutions that are social, political and religious as well as scientific in the narrow sense of the term.

The last point is a significant one. If we are to judge by the standards of the first and second Voyages, Swift's aim in the third Voyage seems to be to suggest the internal contradictions of a society close to the verge of collapse. In Lilliput, where the empire was perceived by its subjects to be threatened by both internal and external enemies, their fears fostered at least a measure of solidarity. In Brodingnag, where the threatening power was wholly internal, a possible resolution was affirmed. But in the kingdom of Laputa-Balnibarbi, the divisions have become much more pronounced. They include not only the conflict between king, nobles and common people, but an even more fundamental cleavage: a cleavage that divides men from women, husbands from wives. Compared with the Lilliputian ministers, moreover, the Laputan rulers seem wholly oblivious to this cleavage, for they fail to share any of the anxieties of the Lilliputians concerning sexual pollution.

53

As Gulliver describes the Laputan 'Nobility, Courtiers, and Officers', they are unable to prohibit even contacts between court ladies and servants (XI, 165), and they have no machinery by which such contacts might be punished. Their failures suggest that opportunities for liaisons cannot simply be attributed to comical lapses in attention; on a deeper level, they are also the consequence of a crucial lack of fortitude and resolution. This does not mean that marital ties are unimportant in the rigidly hierarchical society of Laputa. It means, rather, that there is no will among its leaders to preserve them from contamination. The result is an atmosphere in which Laputan women are allowed a striking measure of freedom; in Gulliver's words, they 'have an abundance of Vivacity; they contemn their Husbands; and are exceedingly fond of Strangers' (XI, 165). They are not granted total liberty, however, for while they are allowed to choose lovers, they are not permitted to leave the island.

One of the aims of this prohibition is to provide a framework within which amorous intrigue can take place in a more ordered and less provocative manner. But it fails to accomplish even this objective, much less to suppress the anarchic rebellion that Swift finds at the heart of the kind of divisions that beset Laputa-Balnibarbi. Gulliver's ancedote of the 'Court Lady' vividly dramatizes the human costs of this rebellion:

> I was told, that a great Court Lady, who had several Children, is married to the prime Minister, the richest Subject in the Kingdom, a very graceful Person, extremely fond of her, and lives in the finest Palace of the Island; went down to *Lagado*, on the pretence of Health, there hid her self for Months, till the King sent a Warrant to search for her; and she was found in an obscure Eating-House all in Rags, having pawned her Cloths to maintain an old deformed Footman, who beat her every Day, And although her Husband received her with all possible Kindness, and without the least Reproach; she soon after contrived to steal down again with all her Jewels, to the same Gallant, and hath not been heard of since. (XI, 166)

Here the 'great Court Lady' remains unreconciled. Refusing to consent to her storybook yet sterile marriage, she returns to her 'gallant'. Swift heightens the tragic nature of her decision by attributing to him all the conventional attributes of defilement: age,

deformity, disease, poverty, despotic violence and a position outside the social system. Since she rejects a sterile purity, she has no
choice but to accept a corrupt impurity and its inevitable, perverse
victory over her person.

The *exemplum* of the court lady illustrates to an extreme degree
the consequences of the sterility that Swift finds at the center of
Laputan culture. This sterility is more than merely sexual, however; it is also social and political – the sterility of a world that
suffers from the rigor mortis of artificial boundaries and narrow
enclosures. When apprised of his wife's return, the husband
receives her with kindness rather than anger. Within this hermeti-
cally sealed community, everyone is a prisoner. As Gulliver remarks, even the king and either of his two elder sons are
prohibited from leaving the island, 'nor the Queen till she is past
Child-bearing' (XI, 172). The ancient symmetrical opposition between purity and pollution – a source of invidious conflict on the
flying island, since it compels the inhabitants to repress passion
and force experience within rigid categories – induces 'continual
Disquietudes'. Characteristically, these 'Disquietudes' are directed
at what is beyond human control and 'very little' affects 'the rest of
mortals'. The threatening power is not something that confronts
the Laputans directly; it has instead been transferred, by an act of
mind, into what escapes their celestial forms. Hence the movement of comets is a possible source of danger in that they do not
conform to preestablished geometric patterns; the sun is impure
because, in its 'continual Approaches', the earth 'must in the
Course of Time be absorbed or swallowed up' (XI, 162). Purity for
the Laputans is geometric form; the impure is irregular form, the
formless, or that which threatens to obliterate form.

This structure of values is indebted to a system of thought in
which science is not as sharply distinguished from magic as it is
today. Thus while it is mechanically inspired, it is also broad
enough to encompass Hermeticism and judicial astrology as well.[1]
Its scientific and technological dimensions have been traced back
to William Gilbert and Isaac Newton,[2] yet it contains elements that
could just as easily have been found in the writings of visionaries
and enthusiasts. The disquietudes which the Laputan speculations
arouse even serve to give their religion a millenarian cast. What the
Laputans fear the most is the 'impending destruction' by the sun of
the earth and 'all the Planets that receive Light from it' (IX, 165).
This millenial tendency is the inevitable consequence of a culture

that seeks to exclude evil and darkness from its visionary realm. The darkness it has rejected returns to haunt it in the fear of an eternal night.

The same union of purity and fear is found in the attitude of the Laputans toward their subjects. Many of the adjectives that have often been used to describe the Houyhnhnms – cold, inhuman, passionless – might be much more appropriately applied to these airborne despots. Where the Houyhnhnms are shown to be capable of living in an uneasy relationship with the Yahoos, the Laputans desperately seek to maintain an authority which depends upon the cruel suppression of others. The symbol through which Swift exposes the destructive nature of this authoritarianism is the flying island itself. Through the operation of this machine, the king and his ministers seek to reduce their subjects to 'Obedience'. The flying island is the ultimate weapon: an infinitely remote, disembodied power wholly governed by the 'magnetic Virtue' of the load-stone. No less horrifying than gunpowder, this magnetically operated machine enables the king to 'deprive' rebellious subjects of 'sun and rain, and consequently afflict them with death and diseases'. The culmination of this kind of strategic planning is the 'last Remedy', a final solution in which the king lets 'the Island drop directly upon' the 'Heads' of his subjects, thereby making 'a universal Destruction of both Houses and Men' (XI, 171). The reluctance of the king and his ministers to undertake this 'last Remedy' is only a matter of self-interest: inasmuch as 'the Island is the King's Desmesne', they are fearful that it would 'render them odious to the People' and thus damage 'their own Estates that lie all below' (XI, 171).

Yet, for all the power which this weapon seems to confer upon the Laputan rulers, Swift's intention in the third Voyage seems to be to suggest the empty authoritarianism of a society close to dissolution. Though the basis for the charge of 'great Oppressions' levelled by the inhabitants of Lindalino against the Laputans is never spelled out, the monarchy is shown to be arbitrary, cruel, rigidly hierarchical, yet in essence superfluous. Riding above its principal cities, it depends upon them, now and then damages them, but never really penetrates their culture. The inability of the king to 'reduce' his 'proud Subjects' to submission through the exercize of the flying island can be taken as a sign of his impotence. Thanks to the inventiveness of one of the 'oldest and most expertest' among them, these 'Subjects' are transformed into 'Citizens' – that is to say, they are encouraged to achieve the kind of solidarity which can only emerge through an act of popular (i.e. 'unanimous') consent and opposition to an hated enemy. Since the king refuses to preserve his power by an act of forbearance, he is forced to accept the consequences of his failure, to learn the hard way how to make intelligent concessions to reality (XI, 310).

But it is still necessary to explain why Swift should have so oddly mixed scientific and despotic features in this satiric utopia. In the first and second voyages, he constructs two contrasting models: the despotism of the Lilliputians and the mixed government of the Brobdingnags. The account is wholly political, but Swift's description of their cultures establishes a correspondence between physical topography and political structure. The same correspondence can also be seen in the flying island, which contains within its very design the seeds of its own isolationism and impotence. It is quarantined in its aerial realm and prevented from moving beyond 'the Extent' of its 'Dominions', or rising 'above the Height of four Miles' (IX, 170). From the start, its inhabitants are cut off from their food supply and stranded alone above a hostile landscape. In short, the Laputans are shown to have developed the typical encapsulated psychology of a court that is divorced from the larger community upon which it must depend for its sustenance. There is thus a definite correlation between its dualism of theory and practice, male and female, ideal form and material body, and the vertical axis forced upon this court by the invention of the flying island.

This vertical structure imposes a very different form of political despotism from that of the first Voyage. Like the empire of Lilliput, the kingdom of Laputa displays certain features that were thought to be characteristic of Oriental despotism: arbitrary power, elaborate court rituals and just that degree of mystification which the underlying metaphysic of its system requires. But where court rituals were used by the emperor of Lilliput as instruments of domination and bureaucratic control, here they tend to immobilize the Laputan rulers within their own precincts. Wholly absorbed in scientific and metaphysical speculation, the Laputan princes are not in a position to occupy themselves with the day-to-day business of government. As a result, this is carried out on the continent of Balnibarbi and lies in the hands of variously appointed and

elected functionaries – the ministers, the politicians and the mass
of projectors whose purpose is to serve the various needs of the
state.

II

In such a context of political division, the relations between different parts of a society seem attenuated, almost nonexistent. Rather
than providing bonds, they only serve to establish the basis upon
which segments can exist in a state of virtual independence. The
continent of Balnibarbi is a self-contained unit, dependent only by
the most fortuitous circumstances upon Laputa for the 'schemes'
by which it seeks to put 'all arts, sciences, languages, and mech-
anics on a new foot' (XI, 176). Just as the geometric purism of Laputa
is the enemy of change, so the 'impure' utilitarianism of Laputa
manifests itself in a restless search for 'new Rules and Methods of
Agriculture and Building, and new Instruments and Tools for all
Trades and Manufactures' (XI, 177).

By and large, the utilitarianism of Balnibarbi is in keeping with
the outlook of its populace. Approximating the perspective of the
English dissenters, they express the very same contempt for
theoretical speculation that the Laputans reserve for 'practical
Geometry'. But cultures that are less concerned with pure theory
than with the material benefits which the practical application of
theoretical ideas can yield are also the most susceptible to disbelief.
If the Balnibarbian projectors conceive of their ventures as unfail-
ing means to prosperity and wealth, like so many get-rich-quick
schemes, others may come to regard their plans as nothing more
than a delusion. This is precisely what occurs in the third Voyage,
where the scepticism of Gulliver and Lord Munodi provides a
corrective to the naïve optimism of these projectors.

This scepticism, however much it appears to underestimate the
satisfactions of material progress, is nonetheless a genuinely legitimate outlook. For it is entirely possible that a nation which em-
barks on an ambitious programme of innovation and reform may
also have to face a period of anarchy and disorder far greater than
any it has heretofore known. In *Gulliver's Travels* this period of
anarchy is defined in terms of myth: the historic myth of the
degeneration of Balnibarbi from its originally pure institutions,
represented by the geographically peripheral estate of Lord Mu-

nodi. Gulliver attributes this degeneration to the reckless disregard of the Balnibarbian projectors for the 'old Forms' of their 'Ancestors'. The consequence of this heedlessness is the deterioration of the material properties of their culture; according to Gulliver, 'the whole Country lies miserably waste, the Houses in Ruins, and the People without Food or Cloaths' (XI, 177). These images of disintegration blur the taxonomic boundaries of Balnibarbi; at the level of material culture, impurity is the wasteland. By contrast, the sanctity of cognitive boundaries is manifested by the reverence which Gulliver and Lord Munodi give to 'ancestral Forms'. The perfection of these forms points to the perfectly bounded and enclosed 'Fields', 'Vineyards', 'Corngrounds', and 'Meadows', of Lord Munodi's estate (XI, 175–6).

If this estate is the social embodiment of ancestral 'Forms', what of the flying island? It would be an error to claim that it is the expression of what is ancient, for the Laputans do not really possess a historical sense. What comes into being and is visible must be subject to a geometry which, because it is intelligible and eternal, exists nowhere in nature or history. Lord Munodi is thus closer to the material world, the Laputans to the ideal world, and the latter is clearly not the more important of the two. For Swift, nature can only be conquered by acknowledging its supremacy and making allowance for its imperatives. In a culture such as Laputa-Balnibarbi, moreover, man must respect the wisdom of his ancestors. Hence Lord Munodi lives on an estate which, though as formally precise in its design as the material possessions of the Laputans, nonetheless represents a link between the living and the dead. Its main 'House' is 'built according to the best Rules of ancient Architecture', while its 'Foundations, Gardens, Walks, Avenues, and Groves' are 'all disposed with exact Judgment and Taste' (XI, 176).

The Laputan inventors are linked to the Balnibarbian projectors, then, by their tendency to give undue precedence to theory over practice, to innovation over tradition. But Swift's satire on technology extends beyond this emphasis to the grandiose scale upon which the Balnibarbian projectors carry out their schemes. The needless destruction of Lord Munodi's mill is the unfortunate result of this scale, for it was through this mill that Lord Munodi had allied himself with the life-giving powers of nature, for the benefit of 'his own Family as well as a great Number of Tenants' (XI, 177). This alliance is ruptured in the project for the new mill, a project that depends for its success on manpower and a cumbersome and expensive hydraulic technology which seeks to challenge rather than to cooperate with nature. The massive scale of this irrigation project is an indication that Swift is also thinking here, as in the first Voyage, of the world of Oriental despotism.[3] Its political dimension is vividly brought out in the moment of panic that inevitably follows its collapse when the planners, unresponsive to the significance of this collapse, seek to save their own skins by placing the blame for their failure on Lord Munodi.

The Grand Academy of Lagado provides a general coordinating framework within which the projectors may conduct their experiments without having to worry about the immediate consequences of failure, but it does not resolve the structural problems inherent in their methodology. Just as the architects of the new mill and canal sought to conquer rather than to follow nature, so the projectors of the Grand Academy attempt by their 'contrary operations' to defy natural laws and limits. Although Swift's hostility to technology seems very broad in this section, it does not, as Donald Greene has argued, necessarily preclude a positive view of science.[4] What is the basis for Swift's positive attitude toward science? It may be sought, in part at least, in his country ideology. For this ideology imposes a definite outlook with regards to technology, an outlook in which people are expected to live on nature's terms rather than their own. By contrast, the scope and ambition of the projects being carried out in the Grand Academy seem to assume the complexity that is associated with the court and city. To live in one place and in large numerical concentrations rather than being dispersed over a wide area invites a perspective that seeks to defy limits, to challenge nature. In this lies the difference between Lord Munodi's estate on the one hand and the Grand Academy and flying island on the other: where the one is situated in a land which is at least partially prepared to support it, the other two are located at the centre of what is perceived as a hostile environment. Nature thus appears as the servant of man, urban and civilized man, the maker of his own culture.

It is this aspiration that is the object of Swift's satire in this part of the third Voyage. For it is the transgressions of boundaries and categories that above all shape his irony. The impulse that led the Brobdingnagians to seek to raise two ears of corn where only one grew before is here placed in the service of experiments that only degrade and defile. For Swift, these experiments carry the odium of multiple pollution. First, they pollute because they degrade some of the projectors – e.g. the begrimed old man with yellow hands and skin. Second, they pollute because they are cruel and injurious to some of the subjects of the experiments like the dog which is accidentally killed by the operation with the bellows. Third, they pollute because they seek to defy the classifications and boundaries of nature. Whether in seeking to extract sunbeams from cucumbers, to reduce excrement to food or to calcine ice into gunpowder, these projects violate the laws by which the natural world is governed. Throughout the section, these natural laws are presented as broadly self-evident: gravity, generic integrity, the irreversibility of natural processes, etc. But in all the examples that Swift enumerates, the odium delimits a specific area of prohibited activities. Within that area, the comdemnation applies. Outside it, however, an alternative science and technology, based upon the exemplum of Lord Munodi's estate, is implicitly being affirmed.

It is probably within the context of Swift's country ideology that this alternative science and technology should be understood. For its main concerns appear to be agricultural, rather than commercial, industrial or military. As Peter Mathias, an authority on British economic history has written, 'agricultural improvement had a more general appeal to the upper and middle classes of English society than any other branch of production' during the late seventeenth and early eighteenth centuries.[5] The extent to which *Gulliver's Travels* relies on this appeal is seen in the verbal endorsement of the Brobdingnagian king and in the example of Lord Munodi's estate. In addition, many of the misdirected experiments of the Grand Academy are agricultural in nature. These experiments are doomed to failure, not because they are scientific, but because they depend upon theorizing which is plainly mistaken, the product of untested and irrational premises.

The intensity of Swift's hostility to these experiments is not due to the fact that the majority of them are mechanical in origin. Like the speculations of the Laputans, they also contain elements that are clearly hermetic or magical in outlook. The *'universal Artist'*, for example, has performed several agricultural experiments which have convinced him that 'the true seminal Virtue' disposing wheat to grow is contained in chaff (XI, 182). Because this occult entity is held to be an ultimate constituent of living things, there is no need for the artist to restrict his investigations to what is susceptible of empirical observation. In the scope of his ambition he thus resembles the nature philosophers of the Renaissance as much as the *virtuosi* of the Royal Society. It is the mystification of his 'true seminal Virtue' which, like the implied magic of some of the other projectors, enables him to sustain his projects, regardless of their plausibility or success.

But if the basis of Swift's attack on such experiments is not clearly intellectual in origin, it is rooted in another attitude also stemming from Swift's country ideology. This is an attitude toward the role of science in society. For Swift's satire assumes that the scientific and mathematical experiments it burlesques have cultural implications; far from being neutral or detached in conception, they are shaped by the same cultural impetus which gave rise to the erecting of the academies in the first place. Thus these experiments are linked, at least by association, to projects that are explicitly political in character. Although these projects are quite different in scope and intention from those of the experimenters and mathematicians, they are located in the same group of buildings and colleges.

In these political projects, the experimental impulse is made to reflect the structural infirmity of the society – the tendency for the divisive effect of its political institutions to predominate over the unifying power of its cultural ones. And once again, Swift's ridicule exploits the Platonic 'Resemblance' between 'the natural and the political Body' (XI, 187); in the School, the human body and its diseases become a primary symbol of the corruptions of Balnibarbian political institutions. The projects reveal a system whose positions of responsibility, like those of Lilliput, are subject to bribery and corruption. There is no real source of legitimacy and no effective protection against abuse. This is the point of a number of projects (the various operations on senators, favourites, councillors and party chieftains) that work equally well whether the intentions of the agents are pure or corrupt. In such an atmosphere of political strife and cynicism, Swift's projects, like the scientific experiments, function in a peculiarly negative, almost perverse manner. Rather than fostering political unity, they provide an inventory of 'schemes' – brain operations, a tax on vices, a raffle – by which the nearly complete lack of unity can be grasped. These projects convey in their mood of pessimism and bewilderment a sense that political legitimacy and unity lie forever out of reach, prevented from being realized by the duplicity of princes and ministers. Their significance is that for the first time in *Gulliver's*

Travels they make political corruption seem endemic rather than a recent lapse from an order possible of being corrected.

It is the same absence of any safeguards against corruption that has turned the Kingdom of Tribnia into a population of 'Discoverers, Witnesses, Informers, Accusers, Prosecutors, Evidences Swearers; together with their several subservient and subaltern Instruments all under the Colours, the Conduct, and pay of Ministers and their Deputies' (XI, 191). The most prominent features of this example are already present in Lilliput and Balnibarbi. So also is the mentality of fear it sustains and which sustains it. But Tribnia represents the most extreme form of this mentality in the four voyages. Here the main justification for the prosecution of spies and plots is a very highly developed, almost obsessively specific code – an idiom of the occult which, though there is no means of verifying it, nonetheless has the force of law. Gulliver describes the main reason for its use by the princes and ministers of Tribnia:

> The Plots in that Kingdom are usually the Workmanship of those Persons who desire to raise their own Characters of profound Politicians; to restore new Vigour to a crazy Administration; to stifle or divert general Discontents; to fill their Coffers with Forfeitures; and raise or sink the Opinion of publick Credit, as either shall best answer their private Advantage. (XI, 191)

The ambiguous use of the word 'Plots' is significant, for it suggests the confusions of a society in which there is no clear distinction between public and private interest, no clear boundary between legitimate authority, the abuse of authority and illegitimate plots and rebellions.

III

Swift has been criticized for the unrelieved pessimism of much of his satire in the third Voyage. It can be argued in his defense that this pessimism is at least partially justified by the objects of his attack. For it is aimed not only at the central issue of the Country opposition – the inability of the nation to preserve its ministers and parliamentary members from corruption. It is also directed at the failure of its princes to achieve the moral legitimacy necessary for the establishment of effective authority. If the implications of this inability have not become apparent to the public at large, it is because of the sentiment and hypocrisy that Swift finds at the heart of the works of 'prostitute Historians' (XI, 199).

One result of this political deception is that the divine right theory of kingship is discovered in Swift's satire to be sheer stereotype. Politics at the highest level of society is seen as differing from less exalted activities only in being more fluid and dishonest. In the political visions on the island of the sorcerors, Swift attacks the patriarchalist myths by which the ruling houses of Europe once sought to demonstrate their moral qualifications to their subjects. What Gulliver learns from these visions is that English and European kings have no real basis for their claims of legitimacy. They have all sought to prove that their political authority can be traced back in unbroken purity to their patriarchal ancestors, whereas the visions show 'in one Family, two Fidlers, three spruce Courtiers, and an *Italian* Prelate. In another, a Barber, an Abbot, and two Cardinals' (XI, 198). Or to put it rather differently, they show that while royal marriages are preferentially patrilineal and endogamous, exogamous liaisons between men of low estate and women of title actually flourished. What this means is that rather than flowing from an originating source of patriarchalist legitimacy, power was actually open to subversion and hence to corruption. Power did not necessarily descend from above, it also arose from below, sometimes from the very dregs of society. This is not to say that it was populist in the Lockean sense. Rather that it was radically and pervasively fraudulent.

One way to think of the political visions of the Island of the Sorcerors is as a *decensus ad inferos* in reverse. Instead of Gulliver penetrating into the realms of the afterlife, it is the spirits who return to the earth at Gulliver's request and answer the questions he puts to them. Although Gulliver 'assumes that they will certainly tell the Truth', since 'Lying was a Talent of no Use in the lower World', their answers are intended to raise doubts about European political institutions. These doubts are not presented as explicitly elsewhere, for when most people read the other voyages, they can accept the characters on the same terms as in any work of imaginative fiction. In spite of the dissimilarity in narrative mode, however, the world projected by these political visions is essentially the same as that of Balnibarbi. It is a world in which secular power has become increasingly divorced from spiritual power.

Many critics have commented on the secularism of *Gulliver's Travels*. In a sense, this secularism is perfectly appropriate for a world in which the social structure has become 'desacralized'. The link between Gulliver's political visions and the recent collapse of the historical, psychological, moral, political, and cultural justification of the European traditions of divine right kingship could scarcely be more striking. The king-and-court, which had once provided a microcosm of the supernatural order, as well as the material embodiment of the political order, are now revealed to be nothing more than a sham. But what makes Gulliver's visions even more pessimistic is the fact that there is no other source of legitimacy which might take the place of the divine right theory of kingship.

The only other tradition of legitimacy to which Gulliver has been exposed is the country ideology that sustains Swift's satire throughout much of *Gulliver's Travels*. But on the island of the sorcerors, even this ideology fails to offer a credible modern alternative to divine right kingship. This is most clearly evident in the sentimental evocation of the six patriot heroes, all of whom are rendered inutile as exemplary figures by their remoteness from the present. But it is also apparent in the reversal of the categories of civic virtue and vice that Gulliver finds typical of modern history. The usual scheme implies a clearly distinguishable separation of good from evil. But Gulliver tells us that he

> found how the World had been misled by prostitute Writers, to ascribe the greatest Exploits in War to Cowards, the wisest Counsel to Fools, Sincerity to Flatterers, *Roman* Virtue to Betrayers of their Country, Piety to Atheists, Chastity to Sodomites, Truth to Informers. (IX, 199)

The same irony thus extends to 'country' attitudes as well as to divine right theory, for the patriot hero is just as vulnerable to the same exposure as the king or counsellor. But Swift is not content to rest in the disclosure that the rituals and justifications of political power are nothing but lies designed to prevent us from realizing their exploitative character. These rituals and justifications are liable to mislead us, not merely by confusing the legitimate with the illegitimate but also because they prevent us from seeing the true nature of illegitimate power. For Swift, power not only corrupts, it is also corrupted, in the sense that it contains within itself the seeds of its own degradation. In the visions, Gulliver discovers that the tawdry low-life creatures who 'interrupt' the perfect 'Lineages' of the royal houses of Europe are defiled as well as defiling. Swift's favourite symbol for this degenerate condition is the diseased and deteriorating human body. In reflecting upon the 'Corruption' that has been caused by the 'Force of Luxury so lately introduced' in England, Gulliver observes

> how much the Race of human Kind was degenerate among us, within these Hundred Years past. How the Pox under all its Consequences and Denominations had altered every Lineament of an *English* Countenance; shortened the Size of Bodies, unbraced the Nerves, relaxed the Sinews and Muscles, introduced a sallow Complexion, and rendered the Flesh loose and *rancid.* (XI, 201)

Degeneration is the opposite of perfection. It is the price man pays for uncleanness because it is concerned with form, countenance, lineament. The 'pox' is defiling because it threatens to dissolve the material essence of man – his size, nerves, sinews, muscles, and flesh. To be afflicted with the pox is to suffer a kind of bodily decomposition. Although Gulliver never makes the connection explicit, what he is describing is analagous to the process of deterioration described in Glumdalclitch's little treatise. For Swift, the end result of this process is satirically portrayed, at the level of culture, in the 'little people' in the first Voyage and, at the natural level, in the 'pravity' of the Yahoos in the fourth Voyage.

IV

The kingdom of Luggnagg represents yet another exotic example of Oriental despotism. Like the Emperors of Lilliput and Laputa, its ruler is a universal monarch, represented in the formal rituals of his cult as the center of the universe, yet, like them, quite aware that he can never be wholly secure in his position of power. The fear that pervades the Luggnaggian court is embodied in the severity of its pollution rules: 'it is capital for those who receive an Audience to spit or wipe their Mouths in his Majesty's Presence' (IX, 205). Like the prohibitions of the Lilliputians, this rule is not exhausted by its obvious aim of punishing a sign of disrespect. It also makes a bodily orifice the symbolic focus of anything that enters or leaves that Luggnaggian body politic. Here the defilement is in part Biblical. The prohibition is broadly related to *Leviticus* 15 and the rule that any secretion or discharge, anything that escapes from the body, defiles. But the prohibition rule accounts for less in Luggnagg than in ancient Israel, since the impure is what departs from the precepts of the king, not God, and for that very reason becomes an instrument of his arbitrary power. The ritual which the king mainly relies upon to buttress his authority is the requirement that his subjects '*lick the Dust before his Footstool*' (XI, 204). In as much as dust, like dirt, is what escapes classification, it is clearly regarded as form of impurity. Thus it can be used as a means of enhancing the king's political power. Since the subject is, in effect, asked to defile himself before his ruler, he incurs the guilt of whichever of his 'Nobles' the king might have 'a Mind to put . . . to Death' (XI,205). Gulliver's willingness to participate in this ritual might seem inconsistent with the knowledge he has just gained from the political visions on the island of the sorcerors. Yet by making Gulliver comply with these ceremonies, Swift dramatizes the true nature of their efficacy. The Luggnaggian ritual of 'licking the Dust', like the parallel Japanese ceremony of 'trampling the Crucifix', not only offers the pretext by which the king exercizes his despotic power. It also supplies the dramatic form through which this power is sustained. Gulliver's servility is living proof that the Kingdom of Luggnagg draws its force, which is real enough, from its imaginative energies, its undoubted capacity to make despotism and cruelty enchant.

There is one group that dwells outside the boundaries of the king's authority and is thus clearly marked out as impure in Luggnagg – the Struldbruggs. The Struldbruggs are segregated from the rest of society both because of their immortality and because they exist beyond the control of the king which resides in his power over the lives of his subjects. But the Struldbruggs are abominable, un-touchable beings in a broader sense, for they suffer the paralysis of those who live between two spheres, those who escape the limits of death but suffer the infirmities of old age. Hence they are deemed unfit for society, their marriages revoked and their em-ployments terminated. The criteria for this system of exclusions serves to bring out their position as outsiders. They are not re-jected for fear of the infection they might transmit to others. On the contrary, they are ostracized because they are losing their

be human: the infirmities Gulliver mentions are linked
ration of the senses and faculties:

> they lose their Teeth and Hair; they have at that Age
> no Distinction of Taste, but eat and drink whatever they can get,
> without Relish or Appetite. . . In talking they forget the com-
> mon Appellation of Things, and the Names of Persons, even of
> those who are their nearest Friends and Relations. For the same
> Reason they never can amuse themselves with reading, because
> their Memory will not serve to carry them from the Beginning of
> a Sentence to the End; and by this Defect they are deprived of
> the only Entertainment whereof they might otherwise be capa-
> ble. (XI, 213)

Incapable of tasting and remembering, the Struldbruggs are no
longer capable of the pleasures by which man comes to recognize
and define his own humanity.

It is probably in this section and in the section on the degenerate
modern Englishmen that, at least in *Gulliver's Travels*, Swift most
explicitly reveals his own disgust at certain aspects of the human
body. For Swift is not employing these examples in a way that
depends upon Gulliver's personal response; instead, he appears to
be using them to attack what he sees as certain inescapable aspects
of human existence. Yet even here Swift's revulsion is hardly total.
In the case of the degenerate moderns, it is directed at what he
perceives – rightly or wrongly – to represent a falling away from
the classical or Renaissance ideal of the human form 'divine'. In the
case of the Struldbruggs, on the other hand, Swift's satire is aimed
at the idea rather than its concrete embodiment. That is to say, it is
pointed less at the consequences of ageing and disease than at the
understandable human attempt to escape death through lon-
gevity.

V

The third Voyage has been justly criticized as an inferior performance. Lacking the sustained narrative power of the other
voyages, it appears to consist of a series of fragments that Swift
may have pulled together from earlier projects.[6] Yet at least a part
of what third Voyage loses in its lack of narrative continuity, it may

regain in the internal consistency of its various episodes and exempla. What unites these episodes is an all-embracing myth of degeneration. Moreover, this myth does not merely link these episodes in an additive series in which the parts are easily inter-changeable. Rather, it connects them in a definite pattern, a pat-tern that is conceived to take place both in space and through time. Appropriately enough, the spatial trajectory of this pattern is downward, a movement from the sky-borne realm of Laputa through the landed demesnes and cities of Balnibarbi, to the nether world projected in the visions on the island of the sorcerors on the one hand and the ambiguous limbo of the Struldbruggs on the other. Equally appropriate, this pattern traces a temporal movement through life to death. It begins with the sterile mar-riages of the Laputans, continues through the abortive schemes of the Balnibarbian projectors, reaches Gulliver's autumnal visions of political and personal decadence, and concludes with the mysteri-ous habitation of a group of beings who belong neither to the world of the living nor to that of the dead.

The basic axis around which this myth of degeneration revolves is a line that divides formal essence from anarchic existence. We can see this line in the opposition between the geometric forms of the Laputans and the crazy-quilt patterns these forms actually yield in practice. We also find it in the discrepancy between promise and performance in the projects of the Balnibarbian academicians, in the disparity between the idealized fictions of the prostitute historians and the unsavory realities they conceal and in the gulf between the promise of immortality that Gulliver envisions when he first learns of the Struldbruggs and the actual facts of their decrepit, decaying lives. In each instance, moreover, the shift from essence to existence is defined in terms of a deviation from a distinctive system of categories and classifications. This is clear enough in the artifacts of the Laputans and experiments of the Balnibarbians: where the former violate a set of primary geometric forms that exist nowhere in nature, the latter defy the laws by which the natural world is governed. But it can also be found in the distortions which are introduced into the ancestral lines of the royal houses of Europe by the introduction of a deliberately random and miscellaneous assortment of low-life characters ('Pages, Lacqueys, Valets, Coachmen', etc., XI, 199). It is also seen in the dissolution of the physical body that has resulted from the introduction of the 'pox' into England and in the deterioration of the faculties of the Struldbruggs. In both cases, the object is man's capacity for pleasure, but while, in Aristotelian terms, one is the voluntary result of excess ('Luxury'), the other is the inevitable consequence of privation (age and debility). These last two examples thus contain a clear hierarchy: the ideal human form – the degenerate human form – the enfeebled body. The last category is irreversible and cannot be altered even by a reformation of manners and morals.

The far-reaching implications unfolded by this panorama of decay are not limited to images of moral and physical degeneration. They can also be detected in the distinctive political model that Swift constructs in the third Voyage. The deterioration of the material culture of Balnibarbi is paralleled by the structural infirmity which isolates it from the flying island of Laputa. The ties between ruler and ruled are seen as inherently dispersive in the third Voyage, undercutting in their very mode the autocratic ideals to which the Laputan nobility are ostensibly committed.

In consequence, the third Voyage presents a very different model of political despotism from that of the first Voyage. In striking contrast to the Empire of Lilliput, Laputa does not disclose the image of a monolithic, 'apparatus state', under the domination of an absolute despot. What it reveals instead is an inefficient, decentralized, composite state in which there are two very different sorts of polity, one centered on the court, the other focused on the cities, country and parliament. The relation between these two centres of power cannot be formulated simply in terms of a contrast between theoretical speculation and practical science, or between court and country. Nor can it be presented solely in terms of an autocratic elite that is contending against the libertarian stubbornness of the inhabitants of its cities. There is rather a sense that the different centres of power, though locked in a divisive struggle, are nonetheless dependent on one another. Just as the Laputans rely upon the inhabitants of Balnibarbi for their food and servants, so the Balnibarbian projectors depend upon the speculations of the Laputans for the inspiration of their schemes.

The dispersive tendencies of Swift's model are reflected elsewhere in the third Voyage. The court of Luggnagg, for example, seems as isolated in its absorption in the ceremonies of power and cruelty as the Laputans are rapt in theoretical speculations. The only other group that is described on the island of Luggnagg are the Struldbruggs who remain encased in their own solitary world.

The interdependence of court and commoners can also be seen in the political visions on the island of the sorcerors. Thus the custom of taking commoners and servants as lovers by the Laputan titled ladies has an exact equivalent in the intermarriages of (male) commoners and (female) nobility that Gulliver discovers to have contaminated the ruling houses of Europe.

The fact that Swift presents two different models of political despotism need not be taken as a sign of inconsistency or muddled thinking. For these models not only affirm the importance of despotism as a theme in the work, but they also raise the dilemmas that this theme inevitably generates. The emperors of Lilliput and Laputa pose two alternative views of absolutism, one arguing for a monolithic, bureaucratic state, the other for political and cultural institutions that are decentralized and fragmented. In presenting these two alternative patterns, *Gulliver's Travels* also anticipates the disputes that have subsequently arisen over the theory of Oriental despotism. The narrative contains the two conflicting views of the ruler that, under the name of despotic and decentralized, still contend with each other today: the ruler as the apex of a highly centralized form of domination and control and the ruler as ritual object, immobilized within his own court and thus incapable of concerning himself with the ordinary business of government.[7] If the latter model seems somewhat obscured in Laputa-Balnibarbi, it is because its ritual elements have been recast in scientific and rationalistic terms and thus made comprehensible to the early eighteenth-century English and European reader.

5

Nature versus Culture: the Fourth Voyage of *Gulliver's Travels*

I

Of all the characters and peoples in *Gulliver's Travels* the Yahoos are perhaps the most vulnerable to a certain style of critical outrage. Thackeray's famous characterization of Swift as a Yahoo – 'a monster gibbering shrieks and gnashing imprecations against mankind; tearing down all shreds of modesty, past all sense of manliness and shame; filthy in word, filthy in thought, furious, raging, obscene' – is a vivid instance of this style.[1] Yet such an approach, while certainly defensible, ignores the fact that *Gulliver's Travels* is more than a vehicle for Swift's misanthropy, and the Yahoos more than gibbering monsters. Indeed the Yahoos are portrayed in the fourth Voyage as a complex social and political organization, not as an aggregate of noisome individuals. And even when the Yahoos are examined as a social group, they are not meant to be studied in isolation, for they acquire significance largely in relation to the Houyhnhnms, to Europeans and to Gulliver himself.

But before we begin to examine the Yahoos directly, we need to recall the way in which loathing is actually aroused in the text of *Gulliver's Travels*. One possible explanation springs to mind immediately. It arises, as we have seen, from the fact that what disgusts in *Gulliver's Travels* is what baffles expection. Why do the Struldbruggs arouse Gulliver's revulsion? Clearly one reason is that they fail to measure up to his preconceptions concerning human immortality and human perfection. Gulliver's description of the Struldbruggs emphasizes that they live in a no man's land between life and death and are not the race of immortal beings he expected them to be. Gulliver's credulity lends the episode of the Struld-

72

bruggs its ironic bite. Were he have to foreseen their actual plight, we may suppose that he would have been repelled by it, yet still doubt that he would have suffered the same degree of abhorrence. The Yahoos can be understood in the same way as the Struldbruggs. From the very beginning of the fourth Voyage, they evoke an intense horror and disgust in Gulliver. Since their 'Shape' initially appears 'very singular and deformed' to him, we might well assume his response is wholly natural, ie. spontaneous and prereflective. But when Gulliver takes the opportunity 'of distinctively marking their Form' (XI, 223), it becomes clear that they defy his expectations in several ways. In the first place they have 'no Tails, nor any Hair at all on their Buttocks, except about the *Anus*'. It is hard for Gulliver to tell what justifies the latter feature, but he speculates that 'Nature had placed' it 'there to defend them as they sat on the ground' (XI, 223). Even more curious is the fact that the Yahoos are capable of walking upright as well as sitting down and lying on the ground. Yet Gulliver believes that they are endowed with 'Claws' rather than feet and are thus enabled to climb trees 'as nimbly' as squirrels. Here is where the disparity between Gulliver's expectations and observations arises, for at this point the Yahoos appear to be land creatures which, though upright, lack certain required physical features (i.e. hair), have claws instead of hands and feet and climb trees and crawl on the ground as well as walk on two legs. We should notice that nothing as yet has been said about their resemblance to men, nor about their filthy habits as scavengers. Thus Gulliver's initial abhorrence appears to be pre-ethical: the Yahoos are loathesome because they fail to conform to any known principle of animal taxonomy.

Gulliver's response to the actions of the Yahoos is clearly influenced by this initial bewilderment and disgust. When he encounters them directly for the first time, it is apparent that he is uncertain of their place in the natural world. They may be either wild or tame animals, predatory creatures or the 'Cattle' of the land's 'Inhabitants' (XI, 224). It is in the context of this climate of uncertainty that Gulliver becomes convinced that he has reverted to a kind of Hobbesian 'state of nature'. In this state, Gulliver assumes that he has a 'natural right' to anticipate attack when one of the Yahoos lifts 'up his fore-Paw', even though Gulliver is unable to tell whether the gesture is the result of 'curiosity or mischief'. The response of the Yahoos, in which several of them 'leapt' up into a tree and began 'to discharge their Excrements' on

Gulliver's 'Head' sustains this ambiguity: they lack courage, yet are still dangerous. They are clearly linked to wild animals by their ability to spring, bound, leap and climb trees, yet they also possess some of the characteristics of tame creatures: cowardice and a propensity to band together in herds.

The reaction of the Yahoos to Gulliver's attack is, of course, an act of pollution, and Swiftian scholarship has often seized upon this act as convincing evidence of Swift's hatred of the body. In a striking departure from this tradition, Norman O. Brown has vividly described the Yahoos' actions as proof of Swift's insight into the way excrement can serve as 'a magic instrument for self-expression and aggression.'[2] But even this interpretation poses a difficulty, for its naive literalism duplicates the Gulliverian credulity that the text is engaged in satirizing. The ambiguous posture of the Yahoos in this scene renders their conduct inexplicable in any terms of simple causation. Indeed Gulliver's own actions emphasize that their bahaviour is more defensive than aggressive, a response to his own unprovoked assault. Moreover it has an exact counterpart in the attack which aroused it – in the sense that it displays the same mixture of courage and cowardice that Gulliver's own use of the 'flat side' rather than the 'edge' of his 'Hanger' reveals (XI, 224). As such, it offers just that blend of servility and bravado which the natural depravity of the Yahoos seems to require. The Yahoos epitomize a depravity whose bravery is inseparable from its fearfulness, whose individuality masks its conformity and which, when translated into human terms, lends ironic point to John Gay's observation that 'of all the animals of Prey', man is 'the only sociable one'.

To attribute a specific structure of values to the Yahoos is not to belittle their nastiness. Rather it is to do justice to the anomalies that govern their relation to Gulliver and the Houyhnhnms from the very beginning of the fourth Voyage. These anomalies are first given a moral and theological dimension in the episode in which Gulliver observes their eating habits. The Yahoos are presented in secular terms, yet Roland M. Frye has shown that they defy Old Testament laws of pollution in their dietary practices.[3] They devour dead carcasses (*Leviticus* 11. 27), including the flesh of dead cows, asses and dogs (*Leviticus* 11.3). But these abominations are only one part of the Yahoo diet. In spite of the (relative) fertility of Houyhnhnmland, the Yahoos dig for roots rather than eat grasses or fruits. Why? Because roots are an emblem of the poverty and deprivation of a species that has sunk to the level of hunter-gatherers. In contrast, the Houyhnhnms are agriculturalists who cultivate oats and raise cattle, thus reinforcing a fundamental Swiftian opposition between warfare and farming, between hunting and agriculture. In a way, the same dualism governs the menu of the Yahoos that characterizes their actions: they are both herbivorous and carnivorous, both foragers and scavengers.

The episode in which Gulliver observes the Yahoos eating provides the context in which the odium which attaches to their appearance and behaviour can be transferred to man. Before this episode the Yahoos had existed for Gulliver only as structurally anomalous creatures. But when he watches a Yahoo meal, Gulliver, to his horror, suddenly discovers his own resemblance to them. Significantly Gulliver finds the basis for this resemblance in their hands and faces. The countenance he originally believed to be that of an animal he now finds to resemble what one observes in 'all savage Nations'; the hind and fore feet he initially regarded as 'Claws' he now sees as differing from his own hands 'in nothing else, but the Length of the Nails, the Coarseness and Brownness of the Palms, and the Hairiness of the Backs' (XI, 230). What is essential is to recognize that these are probably more than merely empirical resemblances; they are also related, for the most part, to food gathering and consuming.

Moreover, these physical resemblances – in which Yahoo and man mirror each other – provide the basis for an elaborate series of correspondences, a generalized allergory. Scholars have sometimes described these correspondences in terms of what is anthropologically primitive or brutish. But the Yahoos occupy a more complex position in Swift's bestiary than this description would imply. For while they may bear a superficial resemblance to a savage tribe like the Hottentots, they are much more vile, as Maximillian E. Novak has commented, than any empirically observed human community.[4] Hence they are probably better described as a logical construct, a conceptual model of depravity. In this model they play the part of an intermediary between two polar classes, predator and prey, between which there is no homology, nor any sort of relation. Suspended as they are in a middle state between the wild and the tame, the Yahoos are neither savage beasts like the lion and the wolf, nor are they domestic animals like the dog and the cow. The Houyhnhnms, who have no natural enemies, stress this point: the Yahoos, they complain, are incapa-

ble of being rendered 'tame' and 'serviceable' (XI, 245). In this
sense the Yahoos come to stand for an element within man that
while not wholly wild, nonetheless resists domestication.
Herein lies the significance of the Yahoos' dietary practices. As
carrion-eating creatures they stand in an uncertain relationship to
grass-eating animals (which live without killing) and predators
(which live by killing).[5] In this intermediate state the Yahoos are
not dangerous to each other or to other animal species as predators. Yet they are dangerous to themselves as scavengers: to act
like a Yahoo is to desire to have everything to oneself. Hence the
Yahoos, though dwelling in a world of relative abundance and
lacking 'such Instruments of Death' as man 'had invented', are
nonetheless shown as existing in a natural state of *'Civil War'*
among themselves (XI, 260). The relationship between scavenging
and foraging is connected with the two possible outcomes of this
internecine strife – the first representing the security and gastronomic well-being associated with victory, the second, the uncertainty and harship inevitably linked to defeat.

Gulliver's discovery of this state of civil war exposes issues that
remained latent earlier in the fourth Voyage. It was easy enough to
distinguish the Yahoos from man so long as their behaviour
seemed purely instinctive. With the appearance of civil war, however, matters become more complicated, since the narrative now
deals with the appearance of ruling chiefs and the discovery of a
surplus that goes beyond the subsistence needs of a community.
Not surprisingly, for the Yahoos this surplus consists of the useless
'shining Stones' of which they are so fond. By shifting the odium
attached to the dead carrion which the Yahoos hunt to these
'shining Stones', Swift attacks the folly of hoarding and thus of war
and injustice. Like corrupted and decaying flesh, they exist as
natural features of the Houyhnhnm landscape. From the dead cow
to the stone, the transfer of odium is doubled in strength. The flesh
of asses at least offered nutrition, but the stones which the Yahoos
seek to hoard serve no other purpose but to engender conflict and
inequality. Consumption and concupiscence are made equivalents
of one another in certain other ways: the Yahoos practice a certain
form of gastronomic gluttony, eating till they are 'ready to burst',
after which 'Nature' points out 'to them a certain *Root*' that gives
them 'a general Evacuation' (XI, 262). Certain consequences flow
from this sequence: the Yahoos establish a strict correspondence
between rewards and punishments and ingestion and excretion.

This correspondence provides the basis for Swift's version of the primal horde which characteristically focusses on the sycophantic favourite rather than the primal father or leader. In Swift's politics it is the favourite, the one who first ranges under the ruling chief, who establishes the pattern of permanent subordination and thus of despotism. The favourite shows his attachment to his 'Leader' by demonstrating his willingness *'to lick his Master's Feet and Posteriors and drive the Female* Yahoo *to his Kennel'* and is rewarded for his pains with *'a* piece of ass's Flesh' (XI, 262). But when he falls into disgrace, he is not murdered and devoured as in the Freudian model. Instead the Yahoos, who are not cannibals, band together and punish him by an act of defilement, not by an act of violence.

This system of primitive correspondences is the foundation upon which Swift uses the Yahoos as a negative model or 'parallel' for human conduct. The effectiveness of this model depends, throughout the voyage, upon Swift's refusal to make the Yahoos 'human', his success in holding them to an extreme conception of what is odious and repellant. Since this conception does not distinguish between the ethical and the physical, it can metonymically transform almost any pattern of behaviour – coquettry, the spleen, gluttony – into an emblem of natural depravity. By the end of the voyage the Yahoos, who were initially presented as relatively simple animals, have acquired a large number of half-human, half-animal attributes.

Yet the relation of man to Yahoo is metaphoric as well as metonymic. Gulliver is frequently called a Yahoo by the Houyhnhnms and in turn calls other men Yahoos. In the vocative the term Yahoo is invariably a pejorative expression or an insult. The point of the expression is usually not the individual but the group, a degraded status that ensures the division into masters and slaves, privileged and expendable. Thus Gulliver calls the fifty men under his command Yahoos when he tells the Houyhnhnm master how he was forced to replace most of them after they had died at sea (XI, 243). Later Gulliver's growing awareness of the 'parallel' between man and Yahoo leads him to identify all men as Yahoos. Gulliver concedes that 'in Shape and Disposition', men are 'perhaps a little more civilized, and qualified with the Gift of Speech', but he insists that they make 'no other Use of Reason, than to improve and multiply those Vices, whereof their Brethren in this Country had only the Share that Nature had allotted them' (XI, 278). Finally even this qualification is abandoned as the term

Yahoo comes, through repetition, to acquire the status of a dead metaphor, i.e. a metaphor in which differences are obliterated in a totalizing identification.

Before the word Yahoo becomes transformed into a dead metaphor, however, it serves as a point of instructive contrast. In the positive sense, Gulliver is described as superior to the Yahoos in the matter of cleanliness and decency. Gulliver also stands in an intermediate position in relation to the Yahoos and Houyhnhnms with respect to food. Although he is obviously repelled by the unclean meats and roots of the Yahoos, he is equally estranged from the Houyhnhnm diet of raw oats and milk. Thus the function of cooking – necessary to Gulliver's survival – serves to place him at an equal distance from the natural depravity of the Yahoos and the natural perfection of the Houyhnhnms.

Yet Gulliver's inability to eat raw cereals carries with it a corrosive irony, for the group evaluating his mode of subsistence is a community of horses. Traits which are taken to be signs of culture and refinement by Europeans are seen by the Houyhnhnms as evidence of physical inferiority. This is the lesson of the Houyhnhnm master who discusses Gulliver's body in terms that are reminiscent of the scholars in the second Voyage. Paraphrasing the Houyhnhnm master, Gulliver reports that he was told

> That my Nails were of no Use either to my fore or hinder Feet: as to my fore Feet, he could not properly call them by that Name, for he never observed me to walk upon them; that they were too soft to bear the Ground; that I generally went with them uncovered, neither was the Covering I sometimes wore on them, of the same Shape or so strong as that on my Feet behind. That I could not walk with any Security; for if either of my hinder Feet slipped, I must inevitably fall. He then began to find fault with other Parts of my Body; the Flatness of my Face, the Prominence of my Nose, mine Eyes placed directly in Front, so that I could not look on either Side without turning my Head: That I was not able to feed my self, without lifting one of my fore Feet to my Mouth: and therefore Nature had placed those Joints to answer that Necessity. He knew not what could be the Use of those several Clefts and Divisions in my Feet behind; that these were too soft to bear the Hardness and Sharpness of Stones without a Covering made from the Skin of some other Brute; that my whole Body wanted a Fence against Heat and Cold, which I was

forced to put on and off every Day with Tediousness and Trouble. (XI, 242–3)

The Houyhnhnm master's account acquires no little irony from the fact that it focusses on the very parts of the body that had originally led Gulliver to discover his resemblance to the Yahoos. But from the perspective of the horses, human nature undergoes a kind of mirror reversal: man is an attenuated replica of the Yahoo, not vice versa.

II

As objects of disgust, as beings which exist outside the boundaries of rational classification, the Yahoos are what is entirely 'other' to Gulliver. From the moment when he discovers his horrifying resemblance to that absolute otherness, there is no possibility of his returning to a complacent, unreflective existence. Gulliver's discovery of the 'entire Congruity' that exists between himself and the Yahoos thus becomes the basis for what is perhaps best described as a complex and secularized version of the fall (XI,258). A consequence of this discovery is that defilement is no longer exterior and contingent upon contact with the Yahoos. It is permanent and comes from within. From this interiorization of loathing arises Gulliver's alienation from the 'Actions and Passions' of his 'fellow Creatures' which suddenly become vile, whereas they had originally been the foundation of his earlier pride and complacency. Estranged from his own species, Gulliver now comes to find its 'Honour not worth managing'. At the same time that the need to defend this self-imposed and specifically human norm becomes hazy to Gulliver, the meaning of human limitation also becomes obscured. A 'desire' has now sprung up in Gulliver, the desire to emulate the infinite perfections of the Houyhnhnms, but this desire has not only 'opened' Gulliver's 'eyes' and 'enlarged' his 'Understanding'; it has also magnified itself, gradually taking total possession of his being. In effect, the serpent's prophecy of Genesis, 'Your eyes shall be opened, and ye shall be as gods, knowing good and evil', now comes true for Gulliver. It is in relation to the knowledge contained in this prophecy that human limitation becomes insupportable, the limitation that consists simply in belonging to a particular species of mortals (XI,258). In fact it is only in the context of this new-found knowledge that we can comprehend Gulliver's observation that the Houyhnhnm master 'daily convinced me of a thousand Faults in myself, whereof I had not the least Perception before, and which with us would never be numbered among human Infirmities' (XI,258).

There can be little doubt that Gulliver's 'passage' from innocence to fault can be traced, as many readers have observed to the sin of pride – not the pride which caused man's fall in the biblical narrative but the pride which encouraged him to view the human species as superior to the creatures below it in the scale of being. It is in the context of this pride that Gulliver's interiorization of his loathing of the Yahoos and 'desire' to emulate the Houyhnhnms needs to be placed. Critics have seen in this 'desire' a second source of pride, yet it also appears to be inseparable from Gulliver's discovery of his resemblance to the Yahoos.[6] As Gulliver himself explains the 'many Virtues of the Houyhnhnms' are a reverse image of the 'human Corruptions' of which he has now become agonizingly aware. Because these corruptions are seen to be real, Gulliver's own aspiration appears equally real.

Gulliver's attitude toward the Yahoos, however, also undergoes a subtle modification. Once he becomes convinced of his kinship with the Yahoos, he is no longer able to view them with the unmixed contempt reserved for anomalous creatures. Indeed, he now appears intent upon confronting the Yahoos, upon proving his genetic relationship to them:

> And I have Reason to believe, they had some Imagination that I was of their own Species, which I often assisted myself, by stripping up my Sleeves, and shewing my naked Arms and Breast in their Sight, when my Protector was with me. (XI,265)

As W. B. Carnochan has observed, Gulliver's attitude in these episodes is no longer 'innocent'.[7] Though dominated by the disgust he had initially experienced, Gulliver's emotions now include curiosity, affection and even desire.

Why are the Yahoos chosen for this internal drama of desire, self-loathing and guilt? It is possible to hold that the instincts of the wild, free, prowling Yahoos have been transformed into the thousand faults of which Gulliver has become aware. But beyond the criticism that a Nietzschean spirit might level against Gulliver's 'bad conscience', the fable points to an anthropological explanation of evil. To Swift, as to the authors of the Old Testament, moral evil is not primordial, coextensive with divine will; its origin can be traced to man himself. Unlike the famous account in *Genesis*, however, Swift's narrative is wholly secularized: evil no longer has any traces of the supernatural but is a parodic mirror image of human nature. But this secularism cannot conceal the tension that exists in the fourth Voyage between the radical corruption of the Yahoos and the transcendent perfection of the Houyhnhnms. Just as Gulliver observes his natural affinity with what may be a degenerate race of human beings, so he views his equine masters as beings who are so wholly above the limits of human nature that they can only receive human obedience. The distance between man and the Houyhnhnms is so great that Gulliver cannot judge them or even comment intelligently on their ways, yet he tries, insofar as he can, to live according to their ideals.

Swift's anthropology, with its assumption that Gulliver occupies an ironic and peculiar position between the Yahoos and the Houyhnhnms, is thus readily accomodated to a secularized version of the fall.[8] As emblems of natural depravity and natural perfection, the Yahoos are equally abnormal with respect to human categories, but where one is abominable, the other is holy. In these terms, the fourth Voyage is perhaps best comprehended as a fable in which Swift seeks to understand the nature of man by understanding how man is related to nature – both in its positive and negative aspects.

III

Is it possible to find a link between this fable of the nature of man and Gulliver's subsequent explanation of European institutions and customs? Actually there appears to be only one such link. This is the connection between the Houyhnhnm master's view of man's corporeal infirmities and Gulliver's account of the 'Art of War'. For Swift, as for Rousseau, the transition from nature to culture, from the animal to the human state is the birth of reason. But if 'Reason will always prevail', as the Houyhnhnm master contends, 'against Brutal Strength' (XI,242), it will pose a much greater threat to corporeal weakness. It is this threat which reason poses to human frailty in the logic of Swift's anthropology: far from enabling him to transcend his vulnerability, man's 'small Pittance of Reason' only serves to magnify it.

This vulnerability is brought out most explicitly in Gulliver's account of warfare, in which man, in effect, becomes a Yahoo to man. Three different usages are concealed in this phrase. In the first place, armies may be thought of as Yahoos and hence expendable. Gulliver employs the word in this sense when he tells the Houyhnhnm master that 'about a Million of *Yahoos* might have been killed' in the War of the Spanish Succession. This usage, however, prevails only when soldiers are viewed collectively. Once the perspective shifts from the group to the individual, the passivity implied in the usage becomes impossible to sustain, for the *'Soldier'* is also disclosed to be a mercenary – i.e. 'a *Yahoo* hired to kill in cold Blood as many of his own Species, who have never offended him, as he possibly can' (XI,246–7). What accounts for the surprising and apparently arbitrary identification of the Yahoo and mercenary is the prominence of the mercenary in modern European warfare. It is in this sense that standing armies were characterized by William H. McNeill as having 'carried into the eighteenth century many traces of their origin from privately raised mercenary companies'.[9] For Swift, the Yahoo-mercenary epitomizes the difference between the militia and the standing army, for he is the soldier whose allegiance cuts across national and regional boundaries. As opposed to an ethic which affirms that it is wrong for an individual to kill a member of his own tribe but is commendable to kill members of opposing nations, the Yahoo-mercenary discloses an actual code of indifferent, indiscriminate murder; in this sense, all wars are civil wars.

The final usage arises out of the fact of death. The body or carcass of the slain soldier is 'Food' to the 'Dogs, Wolves, and Birds of Prey' which encircle it. Since these animals are the natural equivalents to the Yahoos in Europe, their presence on the battlefield becomes an emblem of the complete domination of Yahooism over the scene of war. The Yahoo is thus present in all three phases of battle: as victim, killer and scavenger.

The Yahoo is an emblem, then, of man's vulnerability to his own devices and passions. Indeed, the theme of vulnerability pervades Gulliver's account of the professions as much as it does the Houyhnhnm master's description of man's imperfect animal nature. The usual references to the stock subjects of Swift's satire here, while accurate, is not sufficiently distinctive and does not allow us to place Gulliver's 'discourse' in a specific context. Perhaps the main thing to be said about Gulliver's lengthy condemnation in Chapters V and VI of war, law and medicine is that it is defined by the contrast these professions offer to the behaviour of the Yahoos in chapter VII. In terms of Swift's ironic reversal of the relation between nature and culture, these professions are only superficially superior to the natural behaviour of the Yahoos. Their extreme surface complexity conceals very serious deficiencies and their functional value is actually very marginal.

The example of law is particularly illuminating in this respect, since it depends upon man's added capacity for speech. The Yahoos have no law because they are unable to perform the specifically linguistic act of conceptualization. But how does the law actually work, according to Gulliver? Gulliver's explanation remains within a system of successive rhetorical reversals which, by the repetition of the same figure, keep it focussed on the perfection of the office in theory and its corruption in actual practice. Thus the Houyhnhnm master, much like the Brobdingnagian monarch, is unable to comprehend, for example, 'how it should come to pass, that the *Law* which was intended for *every* Man's Preservation, should be *any* Man's Ruin' (XI,248). Instead of offering a rational explanation of this paradox, Gulliver employs the illustrative example of the '*Cow*', an analogy which links the legal profession to the Yahoos. Rather than providing the focus for a process that will lead to the successful resolution of a legal controversy, the dispute over the cow becomes a human equivalent of the struggle of the Yahoos over dead flesh (XI,248–9).

This is not the only analogy. The uses to which the Europeans put money foreshadow the Yahoo fascination with 'shining Stones'. The portrayal of the medical profession recalls the general image of the Yahoos as scavengers. The same is also true of the treatment of the European minister, which looks forward to the description of the Yahoo leader. What distinguishes these professions from the practice of the Yahoos is the vastly heightened danger they pose to vulnerable man. The origin of this danger lies in man's capacity for speech and hence deceit (i.e. semantic reversals of meaning). It is this capacity for deception which is the 'Quality' that, in the words of the Houyhnhnm master, serves only 'to increase our natural Vices; as the Reflection from the troubled Stream returns the Image of an ill-shapen Body, not only *larger*, but more *distorted*' (XI,248).

Swift's attack on the professions is paralleled by an equally vigorous assault upon the belief that human culture is superior to nature. Although this attack most certainly represents Swift's conviction, it also belongs to a long tradition in which man is compared unfavourably to animals.[10] In Swift's contribution to this tradition, we find a reversal of the perspective in which horses are considered as beasts that are 'naturally' suited for domestication and use. In the topsy-turvy world of *Gulliver's Travels*, they become the masters while the humanoid Yahoos become the servants. And when the Houyhnhnms try to pacify the unruly Yahoos, they demonstrate the superiority of their natural reason by refusing to consider the practices to which men resort in 'taming' wild horses (XI,241). It seems apparent that it is not in nature that Swift found this type of behaviour in animals, but rather in the human mind, in his conception of the relation between reason and the passions. To discredit the belief that culture is superior to nature, Swift repudiates a hierarchy that is sometimes seen as the origin of culture – the optimistic hierarchy in which reason governs the passions as the rider governs the horse. In its place Swift substitutes a hierarchy in which, as R. S. Crane has shown, natural reason (the Houyhnhnms) is only partially successful in subduing the obdurate passions (the Yahoos). Indeed it may be the inability of the Houyhnhnms to govern the Yahoos that prevents either, in this schema, from becoming a culture in the traditional sense. Moreover this hierarchy is in turn opposed to an actual culture – European civilization – in which reason (man) is a slave to the passions (Yahooism) and only serves to magnify their vices.[11]

This inverted relationship between the passions and reason, which is in itself significant, is only the most striking aspect of a dualism in which nature is shown to be superior to culture. In the traditional schema reason is associated with culture and the passions with nature. Swift opposes this schema by affirming a point of view in which both are seen as natural when they are conceived of as isolated entities. In this context they form a hierarchical opposition of perfection and depravity, unity and division. It is only when these opposites are yoked together that they act to undermine one another, thus forming the highly unstable and explosive compound we call human culture. The inferiority of this compound forms the substance of Gulliver's agonizing discovery that man is inferior to both the Houyhnhnms and the Yahoos.

There is one aspect of this pattern, however, which serves to complicate Swift's attempt to demonstrate the superiority of nature over culture. This is the fact that he presents the Houyhnhnms as a community which, though emblematic of natural perfection, possesses a language and forms social relations. Rather than locating them in a primal Golden Age of pastoral ease and abundance, he places them in a Stone Age of rudimentary tools and cultivated fields. This fact alone is significant enough to transform their society from an earthly paradise into a rational utopia. Although this utopia is presented as a model of rational perfection, it employs assumptions which are valid only for certain human cultures.[12]

Why does Swift regard this society as natural? A possible answer may lie in its extreme resistance to technological change. It is this resistance that Lévi-Strauss has in mind when he distinguishes between 'cold' and 'hot' civilizations. 'Cold' civilizations have no history. Resisting all change, including change in the birth-rate, they think of their societies as timeless and time present as a mythic continuation of time past. 'Hot' civilizations are antagonistic, based on a distinction between rulers and ruled; time in them is linear and historical, a succession of the events and discoveries upon which civilizations are constructed.[13] In *Gulliver's Travels*, Lilliput, Europe, and Lagado are ranged, as it were, on the horizontal axis of history; they represent various stages in the development of 'hot' civilizations. By contrast the Brobdingnags and the Houyhnhnms are ranged on the vertical axis of myth; they represent various degrees of 'cold' civilization; where the Brobdingnagian libraries hold few books, the 'Houyhnhnms have no Letters, and consequently their Knowledge is all traditional' (XI,273).

What, then, is the explanation for the deliberately unadaptive character of Houyhnhnm society? The question is not an easy one to answer. On the one hand, there seems to be no reason why technological change cannot be accomodated to a society of virtuous beings. On the other hand, just as the mere presence of Yahoos poses a sharp challenge both structurally and morally to the Houyhnhnms, so the introduction of technology is obviously incompatible with its deepest aspirations.

There is, in fact, one feature of Houyhnhnm society that can help us understand its static (ie. natural) character. This is the absence of fire. In contrast to the relatively advanced societies of the first three voyages, the 'natural' societies of the fourth Voyage are located in a paleolithic world in which the inhabitants lack the one possession that is often used to symbolize the passing from nature to culture. Lacking fire, both the Houyhnhnms and Yahoos know only 'raw' food, but where the Houyhnhnms live on a diet of oats and milk, the Yahoos, as we have seen, are scavengers. It follows that the Yahoos practice a mode of primitive warfare, but lack the technology necessary to transform their primitive conflicts into something genuinely destructive. Hence they provide no real threat to the Houyhnhnms, who are described as being physically superior to them. The Houyhnhnms have clearly learned the techniques of cooperation and the consequent need for political authority. But their power rests as much on appeals to reason as to force, and sustains only as much military organization as is necessary to keep the Yahoos in check. It is true that in order to prevent the Yahoos from over-running the country, the Houyhnhnms once 'made a general Hunting, and at last inclosed the whole Herd; and destroying the Older, every Houyhnhnm kept two young Ones in a Kennel, and brought them to such a Degree of Tameness, as an Animal so savage by Nature can be capable of acquiring; using them for Draught and Carriage' (XI,271). But having restored stability to their land, the Houyhnhnms were contented to revert back to a peaceful life of farming and horticulture.

The difference between 'hot' and 'cold' societies is not limited to the presence or absence of fire. Stemming from the contrast between the vegetarian Houyhnhnms and the carnivorous Yahoos is the further difference in their dietary habits. Where the oats and milk of the Houyhnhnms are 'fresh', the meat of the carrion-eating Yahoos is 'rotten'. In terms of the distinction between raw and processed food developed by Lévi-Strauss in *The Raw and the Cooked*, this suggests a further link between Yahoos and men. If cooked food may be thought of as raw food which has been transformed by cultural means, so rotten food represents raw food which has been transformed by natural means.[14] The parallelism between men and Yahoos can be summarized below:

	culture	nature
raw	fresh	
	(Houyhnhnms)	
	cooked	rotten
transformed	(men)	(Yahoos)

What is so significant about this culinary parallel? The answer is that the conventions of a community decree what is food and what is not food. And since these are social conventions, there must be a patterned homology between the kind of food on the one hand and the kind of society on the other. In the case of the Yahoos, this homology is made quite explicit in *Gulliver's Travels*. Lacking the reason by which they can give their natural inclinations a social form, the Yahoos have been compelled by the Houyhnhnms to become a 'static' society. Yet it is clear that their carnivorous instincts and their readiness to devour food that has been transformed make them into a prototype of a 'hot' civilization. To put it rather differently, their inclinations only require a 'tincture of reason' to turn the Yahoos into the kind of explosive society that Swift describes elsewhere in *Gulliver's Travels*.

The elements which serve to distinguish the Houyhnhnms from this potentially 'hot' society are actually quite simple. On the one hand, they possess the 'strength' which serves in Swift's zoology to distinguish the major categories of animals from man; on the other hand, they display the linguistic capacity which is recognized in *Gulliver's Travels* as the particular attribute of human beings. This union of 'strength' and 'speech' provides the anthropological basis for their 'perfection'; possessing a union of elements that is divided between Yahoos and men, they are equally contrasted with both. Thus they include all conceivable configurations of the original opposition, intertwined into patterns that oppose natural perfection to natural depravity, cultural utopia to social corruption.

V

Purity is the primary norm around which the opposition between Houyhnhnm and Yahoo is organized. Just as the Yahoos are consistently associated throughout the fourth Voyage with nastiness and dirt, so the Houyhnhnms are invariably characterized in terms of 'cleanliness' and 'decency'. But it would be wrong for us to think of this opposition as purely static. Although the Houyhnhnms are portrayed as the 'perfection of Nature', they are not presented as wholly immune to temptation and corruption. Indeed the very intensity of their horror of the Yahoos is an indication of the threat the Yahoos pose to their culture. Representing a strand of depravity within nature, the Yahoos stand for what is imperfectly repressed and at least offers the possibility of devouring Houyhnhnm culture from the inside.

The natural antipathy of the Houyhnhnms toward the Yahoos is reflected in some of the most prominent features of their society. These features almost seem to be intended as a defense against the anarchic tendencies of the Yahoos. Thus the Houyhnhnms place strict rules on sex relations. Where the Yahoos breed prolifically and indiscriminately, the Houyhnhnms rigorously limit couples to two children. Marriage is permitted, and is even required, but is based not upon love but upon principles that prohibit promiscuous interchange. In these and other aspects of Houyhnhnm culture, purity is implicitly opposed to what is formless and uncontrolled. The opposition is two fold. It is conceived of as the result of a balanced and symmetrical dichotomy between physical characteristics and social structures, between nature and culture. The Yahoos are physically egalitarian (i.e. promiscuous and undifferentiated), yet politically despotic. As a social community, they are antagonistic, divided into ruler and ruled. The Houyhnhnms, by contrast, are organized into clearly unequal rankings, yet the naturalness of their hierarchy ensures its stability. Moreover, the Houyhnhnms, who are physically unequal, are politically democratic, governed by elected representatives who meet in a 'Grand Assembly', in which there is no separation between ruler and ruled. Yet it remains to be asked why the system of the Houyhnhnms is so obviously superior to that of the Yahoos? The answer, it seems, is that its natural hierarchy imposes a structure, an order that is lacking in Yahoo society, while its egalitarian polity prevents that structure from breaking apart into the warring bodies described by the Brobdingnagian king. In the ur-despotism of the Yahoos, on the other hand, there is no structure – no nobility, no ranking, no true greatness; indeed, by a perverse sort of logic, it is the most 'mischievous' and 'deformed' who, in this egalitarian desert, is most likely to become the leader.

The anarchic tendencies of this political system help to explain why the Yahoos pose such a threat to the Houyhnhnms. A carrion-eating animal, they ought by rights to have been kept far away from the Houyhnhnm compounds. Nonetheless, they are tamed and used for transportation by their masters, and when they are left alone in Houyhnhnm settlements, they are shown capable of doing quite a bit of material and psychic damage (XI,271). The Yahoos break two boundaries in these depredations: between the wild and the cultivated, and between the clean and the unclean.

The Houyhnhnms, moreover, appear unable to deal effectively with these violations of the boundaries of their world. This is undoubtedly the reason why they are described toward the end of the voyage as debating the question, 'Whether the *Yahoos* should be exterminated from the Face of the Earth' (XI,271) – a fact which may hardly be reassuring but which must be given its due.

Because of this debate, the Houyhnhnms have been criticized as being a bloodless culture, without passion or humanity. But when they are compared with other societies in *Gulliver's Travels*, the Houyhnhnms seem more benign than ruthless. Conquest and carnage are clearly the enforcers of change in Lilliput and Laputa. But the Houyhnhnms have by the end of the voyage been unable to make up their minds to undertake such a programme. Instead they have tried to strike a more humane if ineffectual compromise – pacification and domestication. In order to undertake this seemingly hopeless task, the Houyhnhnms have even given up the opportunity to 'cultivate a Breed of *Asses*, which were a comely Animal, easily kept, more tame and orderly' than the Yahoos (XI,272). Their decision to expel Gulliver seems cruel but is not accompanied by any punitive threats. There is no such ambiguity in the actions of the kings of Lilliput and Laputa. Like the Yahoo leaders, they seek to sustain an authority which depends on the cruel suppression of others.

There is thus a profound difference between the culture of the Houyhnhnms and those of other countries Gulliver visits. The culture of the Lilliputians and Laputans is antagonistic; that is, it seems incapable of overcoming its own divisions; its changes merely give rise to the same sort of conflicts from which they arose. But the Houyhnhnms are 'closely united' as a society. They live together in houses clustered together in villages. These houses may contain a considerable number of people including servants and the aged. Different families are linked together by a system of reciprocal arrangements, in which one couple may donate their offspring to another, should one of their colts die after the 'Wife is past bearing' (XI,268). Corporate unity is also expressed in athletic festivals, where 'the Youth of certain Districts meet' four times a year to 'shew their Proficiency in Running, and Leaping, and other Feats of Strength and Agility'. At the conclusion of these festivals, the 'Victor is awarded with a Song made in his or her Praise', while servants 'drive a Herd of *Yahoos* into the Field, laden with Hay, and Oats, and Milk for a Repast to the *Houyhnhnms*' (XI,270). Finally, quarrelling and strife are conspicuously absent in this closely-knit society; all disputes, except over the Yahoos, being capable of amicable settlement. Because of this normal expectation of internal amity, the Houyhnhnms have no history in the European sense. Resisting all change, time in them is cyclic, measured by the 'Revolutions of the Sun and Moon' rather than a 'Subdivision into Weeks' (XI,273).[15]

It cannot, of course, be denied that the Houyhnhnms, as individuals, seem to lack deep affections. But it can be denied categorically that the pattern of behaviour exhibited, for example, in their response to death reveals an inhuman coldness. The whole point of Swift's emphasis upon the absence of any prolonged mourning ceremonial in Houyhnhnmland can be seen to converge upon the person of the widow who avoids experiencing what would amount to a kind of social death. Instead of undergoing a prolonged period of confinement, the widow returns to the world of the living as soon as she has finished 'consulting her Servants about a convenient Place' where the body of her husband 'should be laid' (XI,275). The point of the anecdote is not that the widow has no affection for her dead spouse; the symbolism involved is social and public, not individual and private.

It is this emphasis upon social harmony that supplies the basis for the charge that the Houyhnhnms do not provide a model for human beings to emulate. Yet while it is true that the Houyhnhnms are obviously prelapsarian in their natural 'Disposition to all Virtues' (XI,267), their material culture is well within the range of man's historic aspirations and attainments. An almost rudimentary simplicity, a kind of primitive technology characterizes their material possessions. Houyhnhnm technology is simple because it is limited by their forefeet to the most rudimentary tools: the 'hard Flints' that 'serve instead of Wedges, Axes, and Hammers' (XI,274). Hence the 'Buildings' that constitute Houyhnhnm living quarters reveal an aesthetic of bareness: large, empty rooms, mangers arranged in a circle; 'Mats of Straw' that are not 'unartfully made' but are 'clean and neat' (XI,229). Simplicity here is coextensive with cleanness; this is made explicit by Gulliver's description of the concentric structure of Houyhnhnm eating arrangements: 'In the Middle was a large Rack with Angles answering to every Partition of the Manger. So that each Horse and Mare eat their own Hay, and their own Mash of Oats and Milk, with much Decency and Regularity' (XI,231). In a general way, an object's production corresponds to its use: the absence of iron is linked to the absence of meat. Both provide the material foundation for the absence of division on the one hand (Yahooism) and the absence of military technology on the other (Europeanism).

Of course the culture of the Houyhnhnms derives from their equine status; but the description of an imaginative utopia is never a neutral idea. To describe is not merely to ascertain but also to evaluate. The implicit evaluation of the Stone-age culture of the Houyhnhnms takes place in the context of its relationship to the practices of the Yahoos and Europeans. Certain aspects of this relationship focus in a very striking way on the opposition between life and death. In terms of this opposition, we find a three-fold system of classification: Houyhnhnm agriculture (means to life); European technology (means to death); Yahoo food gathering and hunting (a middle term since it is a source of conflict but not death). Other relationships deploy a different system of classification: grain-eating animals (the Houyhnhnms who live without killing); predators (the Europeans who live by killing); and carrion-eating animals (the Yahoos who eat meat but who do not kill in order to eat). In sum, these contrasts suggest that the Houyhnhnm society is not meant to exist as a self-enclosed utopia, but is also shaped by its relationship to the worlds of the Yahoos and Europeans.

6

'Not in Timon's Manner': the Conclusion of *Gulliver's Travels*

The conclusion of *Gulliver's Travels* raises enough issues to deserve being treated separately from the rest of the fourth Voyage. A section that includes chapters xi, xii, and *A Letter from Capt. Gulliver to his Cousin Sympson*, the conclusion is a disturbingly unsettled narrative, filtering experience through Gulliver's increasingly exacerbated vision. From the moment he becomes attached to the Houyhnhnms, there seems to be no possibility of Gulliver's returning to a complacent, unknowing self. Yet his attachment to his memories gives Gulliver's character a degree of moral and psychological ambiguity that is not evident earlier in the voyages. Gulliver is unable to reconcile himself to his wife, family, friends or country, but it is impossible to say with certainty whether his misanthropy is the outcome of idealism or wounded pride.[1] The former quality is apparent in his eloquent attack on European imperialism, the latter in the histrionic exaggeration of his claims for the moral efficacy of his travels.

The structural ambiguity of the conclusion stems initially from an equivocation as to the reason for Gulliver's expulsion from Houyhnhnmland. Gulliver's expulsion appears to have no obvious cause and seems in fact so basically unmotivated that it makes him appear like the innocent victim of an unfeeling community. Yet it is the very absence of a motive which serves to underscore the fact that Gulliver's ostracism is rooted in the anomalies of his status as a European and a Yahoo. Gulliver becomes dangerous to the majority of the Houyhnhnms not because of the physical threat he supposedly poses, but because his unique position has made it possible for him to ingratiate himself with the Houyhnhnm master. Consequently other Houyhnhnms stand in awe of him as a rational being. But they also fear him, for he is also a Yahoo, a despised creature whom they have been unable to domesticate. Considered thus Gulliver becomes something like a *pharmakon* – a scapegoat who is expelled for the well-being of a community that is unable to resolve its anxieties concerning the Yahoos.

One result of this political and psychological rejection is that Gulliver turns toward self-exile with all the fierce sentiment of one who has been denied his newly-established identity and status. On the basis of his attitude, we might expect Swift to draw upon a simple pattern of Timon-like withdrawal for the conclusion of the fourth Voyage. Yet instead of developing this misanthropic formula, Swift shows us that it is no easier for Gulliver to resolve the ironies arising from his refractory humanity than it is for the Houyhnhnms to deal with the unruly Yahoos. By finding 'some small Island, uninhabited, yet sufficient' by his 'Labour' to 'furnish' himself with the 'Necessaries of Life' (XI,283), Gulliver hopes to avoid the pollution engendered by bodily contact with his fellow creatures. But when Gulliver is forced into situations in which he must actually deal with his fellow men, we find that their behaviour is far from what his recent experiences might have led us to imagine. On the one hand the 'thirty Natives' he discovers represent the most primitive cultural level he encounters in all four voyages. They appear to be completely unfamiliar with weaving or the construction of permanent dwellings. Moreover the arrow one of them shoots at Gulliver proves in the end not to be tipped with poison as he had feared. Yet rather than displaying the Yahoo-like simplicity that the absence of such rudimentary skills might have led us to expect, the natives are shown to possess fire, the one discovery that is connected in the fourth Voyage with the end of the state of nature and the beginning of culture (XI,284). On the other hand the 'honest' Portuguese sailors are the first representatives of European culture that Gulliver meets. Yet far from showing the malevolence he encountered in his earlier dealings with seamen, they speak to him with 'great Humanity', assuring him 'they were sure their Captain would carry' him '*gratis* to *Lisbon*' (XI,286).

How conscious is Swift's irony here? The fact that the thirty natives and Portuguese sailors display signs of 'Humanity' which the Yahoos so conspicuously lack does not necessarily imply that Swift is repudiating the satiric vision of Gulliver's discourse to the Houyhnhnm master. Swift's own letters reveal his commitment to that vision, yet it is hazardous to assume that he did not see the

dangers involved in Gulliver's self-imposed isolation. By introducing the natives and sailors, Swift appears to reinstate the assumption that Gulliver's discourse had called into question – the
assumption that man is superior to animals, that culture is superior
to nature.

This reversal, however, which is limited to small, isolated
groups of individuals, does not actually restore man to a privileged
position of superiority. At the most it appears to support the
calculated ambiguity of Swift's famous contention, which he advanced to Pope in a letter of 29 September 1725, that man is only
'rationis capax', not *'animale rationale'*.[2] R. S. Crane has shown that
Swift's contention is directed against a venerable explanation of
man's place in the animal kingdom, one that can be traced back to
the *Isagoge or Interpretation of the Categories of Aristotle* of the third-
century logician and neo-Platonist, Porphyry. According to Porphyry, man is distinguished from other animals mainly by his
reason. For Crane, the argument of Swift's letter, like the satire of
the fourth Voyage, is directed against the specific form of pride
which this definition encourages – the pride that springs from the
imagined superiority of man as a species over all other creatures.[3]

Crane's interpretation is important because it helps to bring out
the ambivalence in Swift's argument. Though Swift's declaration
seems to imply the opposite of Porphyry's definition – that man is
only *'animale irrationale'* ie. a Yahoo–it simultaneously renders even
this judgment suspect. In a sense, it is closer in outlook to the
definition of man contained in one of the main sources of Porphyry's *Isagoge*, the *Topics* of Aristotle. Unlike Porphyry, Aristotle
distinguishes throughout the *Topics* between potentiality and actu-
ality, essence and existence: man is defined, variously, as 'intel-
ligentiae scientique capacem', 'animal scientiae capacem', and
'grammaticae susceptimus'.[4] It is true that Swift goes beyond
Aristotle in substituting the much more radical *'rationis'* for 'scientiae' or 'grammaticae', yet he never goes so far as to deny the
Aristotelian distinction between potentiality and act. Indeed, the
main thrust of Swift's argument may be to call into question the
possibility of a deterministic philosophical anthropology, the possibility that there is a single intrinsic property by which human
behaviour can be explained. It is the very perception that essence
and existence are not coterminous that may lead Swift, in *Gulliver's
Travels*, to portray his characters in ways that destabilize any
monolithic conception of human conduct. The mere possibility

that there might be no clear resemblance between the responses of the thirty natives and Portuguese sailors on the one hand and the Yahoos on the other serves to unsettle our sense that the conclusion will unfold in accordance with Gulliver's vision of the irremediable vileness of man. The actions performed by the individuals Gulliver encounters are more complex, more layered than his earlier tirades might lead us to imagine, and the technique of reversal which generates an unsettling sense of disorientation is a faithful translation into narrative terms of this view of mankind.

The underlying ambivalence of this attitude toward human nature is perfectly captured in Swift's comments, in his letter to Pope, on communities and individuals:

> I have ever hated all Nations professions and Communityes and all my love is toward individuals for instance I hate the tribe of Lawyers, but I love Councellor such a one, Judge such a one for so with Physicians (I will not Speak of my own Trade) Soldiers, English, Scotch, French; and the rest but principally I hate and detest that animal called man, although I hartily love John, Peter, Thomas and so forth. (III,103)

This passage has often been taken as a supreme instance of Swift's vision of human nature, a vision that satisfies our demand for both 'realism' and charity. Yet it is significant in another important respect, for it helps to define more clearly the political dimension of this vision. In the name of John, Peter and Thomas, Swift almost seems to call into question the very foundation of the Country ideology, its privileging of public spirit over private interest, of the collective social person over the private individual. For Swift this priority is dubious, since it gives no consideration to the kind of sacrifices which professional groups and communities demand. As he puts it in *A Letter to a Young Gentleman, Lately enter'd into Holy Orders*, 'without weighing the *Motives of Justice, Law, Conscience, or Honour*, every Man adjusts his *Principles* to those of the *Party* he hath chosen, and among whom he may best find his own Account' (IX,79). In any collective body, individual behaviour must be governed by social norms, that is, by the values and interests of its leaders. Only when the individual remains free of partisan interests can there arise the possibility of a situation involving rational choice, in the sense of a decision between the conflicting '*Motives of Justice, Law, Conscience, or Honour*'. Any attempt to evaluate the conclusion of *Gulliver's Travels* should recognize that this special kind of individualism lies at the heart of Swift's vision of human nature and inspires his assaults, throughout the four voyages, on parties, factions, professions and the herd mentality.[5]

No less important as a consequence of Swift's individualism is his critique of the philosophical anthropology implied in the term 'man'. For Swift, this term implies two distinct meanings. The first is the collective aggregate, the total sum of human beings contained in the word 'mankind'. Basic to Swift's contempt for human beings in the aggregate is his deep-seated belief that the 'Bulk' of mankind will invariably be susceptible to invidious motivation, that they can be 'universally seduced into *Bribery, Perjury, Drunkenness, Malice, and Slander*' (IX,79), whereas the individual at least possesses the power to resist these temptations and live according to the principles of honor, conscience, etc. The second is the concept or essence embodied in the speciously flattering definition of man as '*animal rationale*'. What this definition misses so fatally, Swift implies, is any appreciation of the depth of behavioural characteristics formed by collective experience (the '*animal irrationale*' of the Yahoos) and of the difficulty which the individual has in exercizing his '*rationis capax*' despite the counterinfluences of organized social pressure.

This bifurcated approach to human nature is clearly reflected in the double focus of the narrative of *Gulliver's Travels*. On the one hand Swift obviously exhibits a strong belief in the susceptibility of various 'Tribes and Denominations' to 'universal Corruption', and many of the famous satiric set-pieces of the four voyages reinforce this belief. On the other hand, when the narrative shifts from the group to the individual – whether it be in the domestic sphere of Glumdalclitch or the Houyhnhnm master and sorrel nag, or in the public sphere of Lord Munodi and the Brobdingnagian king – the unattractive traits of the satiric object will sometimes give way to the more generous and sympathetic characteristics of the personal subject.

This basically positive approach to individual character is most clearly seen in the capacity for compassion and understanding exhibited by Pedro de Mendez, the 'courteous and generous' sea-captain who seeks to cleanse Gulliver of the impurities he has acquired during his separation from his fellow men.[6] Unlike the nostrums of the professional quacks Gulliver has recently castigated, Captain Mendez's ministrations are intended to be efficacious. Thus he directs that Gulliver should be given 'a Chicken and some excellent Wine' and 'be put to Bed in a very clean Cabbin' (XI,286). Later Captain Mendez encourages Gulliver to 'strip' himself of his 'savage Dress' and offers to 'lend' him in exchange 'the best Suit of Cloaths he had' (XI,288). This suit, like the 'Suit of Cloaths' Captain Mendez later persuades Gulliver to accept, is a counterpart of the garments that initially distinguished Gulliver from the Yahoos in Houyhnhnmland. Confronted with the reluctance of the Houyhnhnms to accept his explanation of his 'false Covering', Gulliver had undergone the humiliation of allowing himself to be stripped naked by the Houyhnhnm master (XI,237). Gulliver's shame in the earlier episode corresponds to the shame he experienced when he stripped European culture of its pretensions. Later, when he is allowed to remain in Houyhnhnmland, Gulliver makes garments from the skins of animals that are indigenous to the region (XI,276). In much the same way that these garments are a measure of Gulliver's acclimatization to the world of the Houyhnhnms, so the new clothes provided by Captain Mendez are meant to provide the basis for the restoration of his dignity as a human being and for his reentry into human culture.[7]

Captain Mendez, the one human being in the fourth Voyage who comes closest to approximating the virtues of the Houyhnhnms, is thus portrayed as an individual, and it is as an individual, rather than as the member of a collective body, that he functions as a mediating figure, leading Gulliver back to the world of ordinary existence. Gulliver's return to his 'native Country', his wife and children is imposed upon him by Captain Mendez. Gulliver accepts because he accepts Captain Mendez's belief in 'Honour and Conscience'. He can look upon men with nausea, yet recognize in his return an obligation to keep promises that transcend his revulsion.

In spite of Captain Mendez's ministrations, however, we find that for Gulliver nothing has really changed. These ministrations are for him inefficacious. They leave him exactly where he was before he encountered Captain Mendez – stranded between two worlds. Gulliver has descended from the rarified atmosphere of a realm of virtuous beings, a realm beyond the reach of human existence. Though his 'Memory and Imaginations' are filled with a vision of the perfection of these beings, this vision cannot insulate him from human contact and from the 'Shame, Confusion, and Horror' which this contact entails. Thus while Gulliver is able to return to human society, he is unable to make Swift's salvific distinction between groups and individuals. It is true that Gulliver continues to find solace in his recollections of the 'Virtues and Ideas of these exalted *Houyhnhnms*' (IX,289), but he is never able to apply these ideas to experience. As a result he remains frozen in a posture of hatred – the hatred of one who is unable to permit himself to become reconciled with impurity.

The view of Gulliver as a comic figure, consumed with his own pride, is not entirely compatible with the 'Shame, Confusion, and Horror' he experiences upon his return to civilization. Still the difference is largely one of emphasis, for in the end Gulliver does become a victim of his own obsession. He does so because the focus of his disgust becomes the individual rather than the group, the human body rather than human faults. Indeed his revulsion is so intense that it leads him to ignore what even the Houyhnhnms had conceded, namely, the superiority of humans to Yahoos in point of decency and cleanliness. The reunion of Gulliver with his wife and children is particularly illuminating in this respect, since they represent the final stage of the transition from nature to culture that was inaugurated by Gulliver's encounter with the thirty natives. Left largely uncharacterized, his wife and children become the unwitting victims of his monomania. Gulliver's decision to live with the horses has often been interpreted in the light of this presentation. Far from being a reascent to a higher stage of existence, it becomes an ironic regression to a primitive state of nature.

The conclusion of *Gulliver's Travels* is thus an enactment of the contradictions of Gulliver's role in the narrative. Gulliver retains his aversion to impurity but loses the social context which gave that aversion a responsible meaning. The distance between Gulliver's outlook and the perspective set forth in Swift's letter to Pope can be measured by his admission that

> I am not in the least provoked at the Sight of a Lawyer, a Pick-pocket, a Colonel, a Fool, a Lord, a Gamester, . . . But, when I behold a Lump of Deformity, and Diseases both in Body and Mind, smitten with *Pride*, it immediately breaks all the Measures of my Patience; neither shall I be ever able to comprehend how such an Animal and such a Vice could tally together. (XI,269)

Gulliver's bewilderment is an indication of how he has lost contact with the moral framework in which he launched his discourse against the professions in Houyhnhnmland. Just as the primary object of human offensiveness is now only man's odor, so social identities and social vices can pass unnoticed in Gulliver's general disgust at the pride of a solitary individual. Even the word pride itself undergoes a semantic redefinition under the pressure of Gulliver's disgust. In the context of his references to 'a Lump of Deformity' and diseases, it loses much of its moral dimension and becomes solely a sign of one's refusal to recognize his physical limitations and deficiencies.

The ambiguity of Gulliver's position at this point threatens to reduce the polemics of the last chapter to a secondary function. It is obvious, for example, that Gulliver's tirade against travel writers is not meant to be taken as seriously as his earlier satire against the professions. Rather it becomes comically self-reflexive: an ironic commentary upon the fictive nature of Gulliver's own text. The more Gulliver insists upon the 'Superiority' of his own position, the more he appears to endanger the moral authority of his argument.

The outlandish nature of Gulliver's assertion of his own veracity relates, then, to the outrageous nature of his own position. In effect, Gulliver has become a prophet of the periphery. Living outside the normal boundaries of social existence, Gulliver fails to abide by the constraints that govern the speech and thought of people who live closer to the centre. As a consequence, he comes to seem increasingly vain and eccentric; far from appearing morally purified by his encounter with the Houyhnhnms, he becomes the embodiment of the bizarre and the unkempt.

Yet, in this situation, where Gulliver, like the legendary Narcissus, is transfixed in fascination before the remembered image of the Houyhnhnms, the argument is a great deal more complex than the effusions of a mere braggadocio. The chapter contains a number of patently outrageous assertions, but it also embodies Swift's attack on imperialism. But the counterpoint does not work here – as it does in the *Argument Against Abolishing Christianity* – to undermine the validity of the argument. Instead it works to suggest by contrast the range of utterance this freedom allows itself and the penetration it achieves. C. J. Rawson has observed that it is precisely because Gulliver is eccentric that he continues to remain a potent satirist, a 'raging recluse'.[8] What is insisted upon is his enduring gullibility, the gullibility that allows him to exculpate the 'British' from his general indictment of European imperialism. But Gulliver's naivete does not preclude his moral authority as a peripheral prophet but assures it, since without it, his candour in attacking the centre would seem implausible. And Swift takes full advantage of this mixture of naivete and candour, using it to insist upon connections of which Gulliver is only partially aware. One such connection, for example, is the resemblance, only implicit in Gulliver's indictment, between travel writers and the 'Pyrates' who invade other countries. Just as the former impose 'the grossest Falsities on the unwary Reader', so the latter take advantage of the 'Kindness' of 'an harmless People'. At this point in the interpretation suggested by Swift, the proper meaning of the parallel is clear enough: the falsehoods of travel writers are generically akin to the falsehoods of the 'prostitute Historians' Gulliver condemns on the island of Glubbdubdrib. If the one has ascribed 'the greatest exploits in War to cowards', so the other, by implication, has attributed the greatest humanity to 'Pyrates'.

Gulliver's conclusion is that it was the opportunism of 'Pyrates', thinly disguised as patriotic actions, that first showed European princes how to enslave foreign peoples. For their piratical violation of the laws of reciprocity provided the nucleus for the much broader violation of the laws of retributive justice – the 'free License given to all Acts of Inhumanity and Lust' – that occurred in subsequent invasions. The common characteristic of these invasions was that cultural frontiers were overrun, 'Natives . . . driven out', and 'Princes tortured to discover Gold' (XI,294). Christianity served as a significant historical function in this process of extermination, for it provided European rulers with an ideological justification for the depredations of their military forces; they were a *'modern Colony* sent to convert and civilize an idolatrous and barbarian People' (XI,294).

What needs to be emphasized is the impact of this attack on imperialism upon Gulliver's identification of men and Yahoos. For it stands in sharp contrast to the colonialist ideology in which primitive peoples, like the Hottentots, are seen as symbols of the Fall and Original Sin. In the diaries and sermons of John Wesley, for instance, Africans and other native groups occupy a place virtually analogous to that of the Yahoos. 'To compare [these groups] with horses or any of our domestic animals', he once wrote, 'would be doing them too much honour'.[9] In Gulliver's satire, by contrast, such a comparison becomes difficult, if not impossible, for it is the conquerors, not the conquered, who are castigated for their Yahooism. If the weakness and naivete of foreign nations are enough to endanger the customs and institutions upon which their cultures are based, then no one can ever be free from domination by members of his own kind. The parallel with the 'Buccaneers' who seize Gulliver's ship at the beginning of the fourth Voyage is all-too-apparent, and in one case as in the other, the ruthlessness with which the helpless are subjugated leads to the belief that it is the will to dominate of the oppressor, not the cultural backwardness of the oppressed, that reduces man to a state lower than that of the brutes.

In this way the last chapter becomes a recapitulation of earlier themes in *Gulliver's Travels*. Gulliver's indictment of the plundering of foreign nations recalls his earlier attack on European warfare. Likewise his exposure of the fictions that sustain these colonizing adventures brings to mind his earlier unmasking of the fictions underlying the royal houses of Europe. But this recapitulation is not only concerned with the positive dimension of Gulliver's earlier discoveries. Gulliver's exculpation of the 'British Nation' from his critique of colonialism resembles his panegyric of the British institutions to the Brobdingnagian king. Swift's point is not so much to undermine Gulliver's authority or to reveal his failure to learn from his errors as it is to demonstrate the persistence of his major themes. Dwelling on the periphery, Gulliver has become more vain and eccentric, but he remains the same character who provided the vehicle for Swift's earlier attacks.

What are we to make of the significance of this vivid recapitulation of earlier themes for Gulliver's character? Is he a tragic hero who has seen a vision of perfection? Or is he a comic figure, containing within himself the seeds of the pride that undermines his moral authority? These two conflicting interpretations are not necessarily at cross purposes, for it is entirely possible that Swift allows for both answers, that an essential aim of his satire is to cultivate a certain indeterminacy of meaning. If this argument is valid, the meaning of the text – perhaps in contrast to that of most satiric works – is conceived of as self-consciously elusive, always contingent upon the possibility of further dialectical reversals, further shifts in judgment. Lest we suppose that this explanation is only a kind of evasion, another version of the Augustan compromise, we should realize that it is entirely consistent with Swift's critical principles. As a means of avoiding the dogmatism implicit in his rule that 'Satyr is a sort of *Glass*, wherein Beholders do generally discover every body's Face but their Own', it is entirely appropriate that the ultimate significance of Gulliver's stance toward his fellow men at the end of the fourth Voyage should never be entirely resolved.

Notes

CHAPTER 1: INTRODUCTION

1. The classical statement of this position can be found in Deane Swift, *An Essay upon the Life, Writings, and Character of Dr. Jonathan Swift* (London, 1781), rpt. in *A Casebook on Gulliver among the Houyhnhnms*, ed. Milton P. Foster (New York: Crowell, 1961) pp. 74–6. Among modern interpretations of Swift from this perspective, one might cite T. O. Wedel, 'On the Philosophical Background of *Gulliver's Travels*', *SP*, XXIII (1926) 434–50; and Louis A. Landa, 'Jonathan Swift', *English Institute Essays: 1946* (New York: Columbia University Press, 1946) pp. 20–35. The most extreme attempts to examine *Gulliver's Travels* from a Christian point of view are Martin Kallich's *The Other Side of the Egg: Religious Satire in Gulliver's Travels* (Bridgeport, Conn.: Conference on British Studies, 1970); and L. J. Morrissey's *Gulliver's Progress* (Hamden, Conn.: Archon Books, 1978).
2. This argument can be traced back to John Boyle, fifth Earl of Orrery, *Remarks on the Life and Writings of Dr. Jonathan Swift* (London: 1752), rpt. in *A Casebook on Gulliver among the Houyhnhnms*, pp. 71–3; and William Makepeace Thackeray, *English Humourists of the Eighteenth Century*, eds. J. W. Cunliffe and H. A. Watt (Chicago and New York: Scott Foresman, 1911) pp. 50–8. Influential modern versions of this perspective are those of Aldous Huxley, *Do What You Will* (Garden City, New York: Doubleday Doran, 1911) pp. 99–114; and John Middleton Murry, *Jonathan Swift: a Critical Biography* (New York: Noonday Press, 1955) pp. 432–8.
3. Mary Douglas, *Purity and Danger: an Analysis of the Concepts of Pollution and Taboo* (London, [etc.]: Routledge & Kegan Paul, 1966) p. 41. Peter Steele remarks in passing that Mary Douglas's study 'might furnish us with matter for a great deal of speculation' in connection with Swift, *Jonathan Swift: Preacher and Jester* (Oxford: Clarendon Press, 1978) p. 27.
4. Paul Ricoeur, *The Symbolism of Evil* (New York, [etc.]: Harper & Row, 1967) p. 27.
5. F. R. Leavis, 'Swift's Negative Irony', *The Common Pursuit* (London: Chatto & Windus, 1952), rpt. in *Gulliver's Travels*, ed. Robert A. Greenberg (New York: Norton, 1970) p. 422.
6. Jean Alexander, 'Yeats and the Rhetoric of Defilement', *REL*, VI (1965) 44–57, locates Swift in a tradition of defilement that includes Spenser, Milton, Marvell, and Baudelaire, but while her approach shifts the

focus from an expressive to a rhetorical perspective, it still confirms the conventional view, i.e. Swift's intention 'is to inspire disgust for the human body and acts of the body. The effect is primarily sexual revulsion' (p. 46).

7. *Gulliver's Travels*, 1726 (rev. edn, 1959), ed. Herbert Davis, in *The Prose Works of Jonathan Swift*, 14 vols (Oxford: Basil Blackwell, 1939–68) XI, 29. All citations to *Gulliver's Travels* in my text are to this edition.

8. William Dampier, *A New Voyage Around the World* (London, 1703); Edward Cooke, *A Voyage to the South Sea, and Around the World* (London, 1712), and Woodes Rogers, *A Cruising Voyage Round the World* (London, 1712), all rpt. in *Robinson Crusoe*, ed. Michael Shinagle (New York: Norton, 1975) pp. 245–53. R. W. Frantz, *The English Traveller and the Movement of Ideas, 1660–1732* (Lincoln: University of Nebraska Press, 1967) pp. 67–8, distinguishes broadly between the narrative of detached observation and the 'narrative of authentic adventure'. In the latter accounts, writes Frantz, objective presentation is 'repeatedly thrust into the background by the imperious authority of '"imminent escapes' and 'Strange Surprizing Adventures"' (p. 68).

9. *The Rites of Passage* (1908), cited from *Purity and Danger*, p. 96.

10. Jenny Mezciems observes that throughout *Gulliver's Travels* Swift employs the term fortune in two distinct senses, one passive, the other active 'The Unity of Swift's "Voyage to Laputa": Structure and Meaning in Utopian Fiction', *MLR*, LXXII (1977) 13, 14.

11. The view that Gulliver is the primary object of Swift's satire in the four voyages usually takes two forms, one seeing him as a physical victim, the other as an unreliable narrator and observer. For an example of the former, see Paul Fussell, Jr., 'The Frailty of Lemuel Gulliver', in *Essays in Literary History*, eds Rudolf Kirk and C. F. Main (New Brunswick, NJ: Rutgers University Press, 1960) pp. 113–25. For examples of the latter, see Hugo M. Reichard, 'Gulliver the Pretender', *PLL*, I (1965) 316–22; Jon S. Lawry, 'Dr. Lemuel Gulliver and "the Thing which was not"', *JEGP*, LXVII (1968) 212–34; and Robert M. Philmus,'Swift, Gulliver and the Thing which was not', *ELH*, XXXVIII (1971) 62–79. A strategy for giving Gulliver a positive role in terms that are consistent with the conventions of the modern novel is to trace his growing self-knowledge throughout the four voyages. See, e. g. John H. Sutherland, 'A Reconsideration of Gulliver's Third Voyage', *SP*, LIV (1957) 45–52; and Edmund Reiss, 'The Importance of Swift's Glubbdubdrib Episode', *JEGP*, LIX (1960) 223–8. The tendency of my approach is to concentrate on the way Gulliver functions in each voyage when it is considered as a distinct narrative unit.

12. *Swift: Poetical Works*, ed. Herbert Davis (London, [etc.]: Oxford University Press, 1967) p. 86.

13. Claude Lévi-Strauss, *From Honey to Ashes: Introduction to a Science of Mythology*, II (London: Cape, 1973) p. 383.

14. 'Swift's Fallen City: "A Description of the Morning"', in *The World of Jonathan Swift*, ed. Brian Vickers (Cambridge, Mass.: Harvard University Press, 1968) pp. 171–94.

CHAPTER 2: THE FIRST VOYAGE

1. Like many of the pollution rules in *Gulliver's Travels*, this prohibition can be traced back to Scripture (*Deuteronomy.* 23.10–15). At the same time, Swift would have found many instances of prohibitions and rites governing purity and impurity in the literature of exotic travel. See, for example, *The Six Voyages of John Baptista Tavernier* (2 vols, London, 1678) I, 167, 168, 236, 237. Sir John Chardin often adopts a detached and ironic attitude toward the pollution rules of foreign lands, noting, for example, that the Persians 'would turn a League out of the way to avoid a Bodily Pollution', yet show 'little Honesty', *A New and Accurate Description of Persia and other Eastern Nations* (2 vols, London, 1724); rpt. as *Sir John Chardin's Travels in Persia*, II (London: The Argonaut Press, 1827) p. 187. Montesquieu's *Persian Letters* (1721) also contains numerous references to purity and defilement, many of them obviously ironic: Letters, 17, 18, 26, 48, 93.

2. On Swift's general interest in Plato, see Irene Samuel, 'Swift's Reading of Plato', *SP*, LXXIII (1976) 440–62; and Hoyt Trowbridge, 'Swift and Socrates', in *From Dryden to Jane Austen* (Albuquerque: University of New Mexico Press, 1977) pp. 81–123. John F. Reichert, 'Plato, Swift and the Houyhnhnms', *PQ*, XLVII (1968) 179–92, establishes a number of convincing parallels between Plato's *Republic* and the society of the Houyhnhnms in the fourth Voyage.

3. *Purity and Danger*, p. 128.

4. *Ibid.*, p. 124.

5. J. A. Downie, 'Political Characterization in *Gulliver's Travels*', *Yearbook of English Studies*, VII (1977) pp. 108–20, applies this term to the position adopted by the Brobdingnagian king in his conversations with Gulliver, but it can easily be extended to the general political *ethos* of the work as a whole. See also H. T. Dickinson, *Liberty and Property: Political Ideology in Eighteenth-Century Britain* (New York: Holmes and Meier, 1977) pp. 163–94.

6. Ricardo Quintana, *Swift: an Introduction* (London: [etc.]: Oxford University Press, 1955) p. 147; G. Wilson Knight, 'Swift and the Symbolism of Irony', in *The Burning Oracle* (London: Oxford University Press, 1939); rpt. in *Gulliver's Travels*, ed. Greenberg, p. 384.

7. J. P. W. Rogers, 'Swift, Walpole and the Rope Dancers', *PLL*, VIII (1972) 159–71, explores the relation of the rope dancers to contemporary English popular entertainments, most notably pantomime.

8. William H. McNeill, *The Pursuit of Power: Technology, Armed Force and Society since A.D. 1000* (Chicago: University of Chicago Press, 1982) pp. 125–39.

9. F. P. Lock, *The Politics of Gulliver's Travels* (Oxford: Clarendon Press, 1980) p. 89. Earlier versions of this argument are to be found in Phillip Harth, 'The Problem of Political Allegory in *Gulliver's Travels*', *MP*, LXXIII (1976) 540–7; and J. A. Downie, 'Political Characterization in *Gulliver's Travels*', op. cit., pp. 108–20.

10. Lock briefly notes the Asiatic character of Lilliputian despotism (*The Politics of Gulliver's Travels*, p. 129).

11. *Miscellaneous and Autobiographical Pieces, Fragments and Marginalia*, ed. Herbert Davis, in *The Prose Works of Jonathan Swift*, 14 vols (Oxford: Basil Blackwell, 1939–1968) v, 100.

12. For accounts of this familiar feature of Oriental despotism, see. e. g. Herodotus, *The History*, 2 vols (London: Dent, [etc.], 1910) I, 70; Tavernier, *Travels in India*, II, 291; and Chardin, *Sir John Chardin's Travels in Persia*, I, 85, 86.

13. Karl A. Wittfogel, *Oriental Despotism: a Comparative Study of Total Power* (New Haven, Conn.: Yale University Press, 1957). Wittfogel traces the notion of a specific category of 'semi-Asiatic' despotism back to Marx and Engels (p. 5).

14. Charles de Secondat, Baron de La Brède et de Montesquieu, *The Persian Letters*, ed. and tr. by J. Robert Loy (New York: Meridian Books, 1961), Letter 37, pp. 95–6. See also Letter 131. For further information concerning the prevalence of the notion of Oriental despotism during the period, see Pierre Martino, *L'Orient dans la Litterature Française au XVIIᵉ et au XVIIIᵉ Siècle* (Paris: Hachette, 1906) pp. 324–7.

15. Geoffrey Holmes, *The Professions and Social Change in England, 1680–1730* (London: Oxford University Press, 1979), establishes the existence of such a state-directed bureaucracy in early eighteenth-century England. According to Holmes, by 1710 the English civil service had grown to over 11000, including 4000 army officers. 'Once this great edifice of state-employed professionals had been erected', Holmes concludes, 'it proved extremely difficult to dismember' (p. 324).

CHAPTER 3: THE BROBDINGNAGIAN KING

1. Charles Cotton, *Poems*, ed. John Beresford (New York: n.d.) and Thomas Burnet, *Sacred Theory of the Earth* (London, 1684); both cited by Marjorie Hope Nicolson, *Mountain Gloom and Mountain Glory: the Development of the Aesthetics of the Infinite* (Ithaca, NY: Cornell University Press, 1959) pp. 66–7, 198.

2. On the 'microscopic eye', see, e.g. John Locke, *An Essay Concerning Human Understanding*, Book II, ch. 23; and Alexander Pope, *An Essay on Man*, Epistle I, ll. 193–4. A fuller discussion of this theme can be found in the footnote to the Maynard Mack edition of *An Essay on Man* (London: Methuen, 1950). See Edward Wasiolek, 'Relativity in *Gulliver's Travels*', *PQ*, 38 (1958) 110–16; and Carole Fabricant, *Swift's Landscape*, (Baltimore and London: Johns Hopkins University Press, 1982) pp. 180–1, for philosophical and literary discussions of Swift's manipulations of perspective.

3. Kathleen Williams, *Jonathan Swift and the Age of Compromise* (Lawrence, KS: University of Kansas Press, 1967) pp. 156–7.

4. For a more specific discussion of the historiographical debate of the 1720s, see Isaac Kramnick, *Bolingbroke and His Circle: The Politics of*

Nostalgia in the Age of Walpole (Cambridge, Mass.: Harvard University Press, 1968) pp. 127–36.

5. *Liberty and Property*, pp. 163–9. On Swift's adherence to the principles of mixed government, see also Z. S. Fink, 'Political Theory in Gulliver's Travels', *ELH*, XIV (1947) 151–61; and Myrrdin Jones, 'Swift, Harrington, and Corruption in England', *PQ*, LIII (1974) 59–70. These articles, while offering valuable insights into Swift's ideology, suffer from the fact that they tend to concentrate exclusively on the views of the Brobdingnagian king. By failing to notice the extent to which Gulliver shares many of these views, they tend to overlook the more sceptical and pessimistic aspects of the king's interrogation.

6. This discussion is indebted to the theory of parasitism advanced by Anatol Rapoport in *Fights, Games and Debates* (Ann Arbor, Mich.: University of Michigan Press, 1960) pp. 67, 68.

7. 'Swift, Harrington, and Corruption in England', op. cit., pp. 69–70. Jones recognizes that Swift opposes Harrington in *The Contests and Dissensions in Athens & Rome* (1701).

8. *The Social Contract*, I, 7.

9. Irvin Ehrenpreis, 'History', in *The Personality of Jonathan Swift*, (Cambridge, Mass.: Harvard University Press, 1958) pp. 64, 65.

10. For other discussions of Swift's view of history besides that of Ehrenpreis, see James William Johnson, 'Swift's Historical Outlook', *Journal of British Studies*, IV (1965) 52–67; and F. P. Lock, *The Politics of Gulliver's Travels*, pp. 33–65. In examining Swift's historical outlook, we should always be careful to distinguish two distinct kinds of historical writing: the 'serious' history of works like *An Enquiry into the Behavior of the Queen's Last Ministry* and the ironic, sceptical, revisionist history of *A Tale of a Tub*, *Gulliver's Travels* and some of Swift's more aggressively polemical works.

11. Jeffrey Hart, 'The Ideologue as Artist: Some Notes on *Gulliver's Travels*', *Criticism*, II (1960) 125–33, discusses the relation between past and present as a central structural principle in *Gulliver's Travels*.

12. *An Enquiry into the Behavior of the Queen's Last Ministry*, ed. Irvin Ehrenpreis (Bloomington, Ind.: Indiana University Press, 1956), p. 3.

CHAPTER 4: THE SYSTEM AT WAR WITH ITSELF

1. Paul J. Korshin, 'The Intellectual Context of Swift's Flying Island', *PQ*, L (1971) 638–46, provides an illuminating study of the intellectual background of this strange mixture of science, magic and superstition.

2. See, especially, Marjorie Hope Nicolson and Nora M. Mohler, 'Swift's "Flying Island" in the Voyage to Laputa', *Annals of Science*, II (1937) 405–30. Even though Swift's satire is aimed at the speculative traditions of European science, sources for the geometrizing impulse of the Laputan rulers can also be found in the literature of exotic travel. In Tavernier's *Travels in India*, for instance 'every *Bramin*' is de-

scribed as having 'his Magick Book, wherein are abundance of Circles and Semicircles, Squares, Triangles, and several sorts of Cisers' (*The Six Voyages of John Baptista Tavernier* [London, 1678], I, 179, 180). In subsequent passages, the Bramins are shown using these geometric forms in a variety of shamanistic contexts:

3. Wittfogel makes hydraulic agriculture the organizing structural principle of Oriental despotism (op. cit., *passim*). Pat Rogers, 'Gulliver and the Engineers', *MLR*, LXX (1975) 260–70, links the collapse of this project to the South Sea Bubble.

4. Donald Greene, 'Swift: Some Caveats', *Studies in the Eighteenth-Century: II*, ed. R. F. Brissenden (Toronto: University of Toronto Press, 1973) 356–8. For an illuminating study of the close relation between these projects and contemporary experiments described in the *Transactions of the Royal Society*, see Marjorie Hope Nicolson and Nora M. Mohler, 'The Scientific Background of Swift's *Voyage to Laputa*', *Annals of Science*, II (1937) 299–334.

5. Peter Mathias, 'Who Unbound Prometheus? Science and Technological Change, 1600–1800', in *The Transformation of England: Essays in the Economic and Social History of England in the Eighteenth Century* (New York: Columbia University Press, 1979) p. 81.

6. There have been several recent attempts to defend the thematic and structural unity of the third Voyage: Edmund Reiss, 'The Importance of Swift's Glubbdubdrib Episode', *JEGP*, LIX (1960) 223–8; J. K. Walton, 'The Unity of the Travels', *Hermanathena*, CIV (1967) 5–50; and Jenny Mezciems, 'The Unity of Swift's "Voyage to Laputa": Structure and Meaning in Utopian Fiction', *MLR*, LXXII (1977) 1–21.

7. Controversy over Wittfogel's theory of Oriental despotism is ongoing. Generally speaking, critics oppose Wittfogel by establishing the existence in Asia of radically decentralized and segmentary polities rather than the monolithic apparatus states Wittfogel described. See, e. g. Dennis Twitchett, 'Some Remarks on Irrigation under the T'Ang', *T'Oung Pao*, XLVIII (1958) 175–94; and Clifford Geertz, *Negara: The Theatre State in Nineteenth-Century Bali* (Princeton, NJ: Princeton University Press, 1980). Marshall Sahlins sees two opposing tendencies at work in all primitive societies, one centrifugal and centralizing, the other centripetal and dispersive (*Stone Age Economics* [Chicago and New York: Aldine, Atherton, 1972], p.131).

CHAPTER 5: NATURE VERSUS CULTURE

1. *Thackeray's English Humorists of the Eighteenth Century*, p. 56.

2. Norman O. Brown, 'Swift's Excremental Vision', *Life Against Death, the Psychoanalytical Meaning of History* (New York: Vintage, 1959) pp. 189–92. Of the other two examples of the Yahoo use of excrement as a symbol of aggression that Brown cites, one describes a simple defence mechanism that is found in children and many animals: 'While I held the odious Vermin in my Hands, it voided its filthy Excrements of a

yellow liquid Substance, all over my Cloaths' (XI, 66). The other is the only instance in the fourth Voyage in which the Yahoos can actually be said to use excrement as a symbol of aggression, but even here it is used in a very specific context: 'his Successor, at the Head of all the *Yahoos* in that District, Young and Old, Male and Female, come in a Body, and discharge their Excrements upon him from Head to Foot' (XI, 263).

3. Roland Mushat Frye, 'Swift's Yahoo and the Christian Symbols for Sin', *JHI*, XV (1954) 201–17. Frye's thesis examined critically by W. A. Murray in 'Mr. Roland M. Frye's Article on Swift's Yahoo', *JHI*, XV (1954) 599–601. John M. McManmon, 'The Problem of a Religious Interpretation of *Gulliver's Travels*', *JHI*, XXVII (1966) 59–72, subjects the Christian interpretation of *Gulliver's Travels* to a rigorous critique.

4. *The Wild Man Within: an Image in Western Thought from the Renaissance to Romanticism*, eds. Edward Dudley and Maximilian E. Novak (Pittsburgh: University of Pittsburgh Press, 1972) p. 212. On the Hottentots as a possible source for the Houyhnhnms, see R. W. Frantz, 'Swift's Yahoo and the Voyagers', *MP*, XXIX (1931) 49–57. Another, more clearly literary source for the Yahoos might be one of the 'devilish creatures' that Defoe depicts in *Captain Singleton*. Though much cruder than a Yahoo, this creature is described as structurally anomalous, borne of 'an ill-gendered kind, between a tiger and a leopard' (*Captain Singleton* [New York: Crowell, 1903], pp. 134–5).

5. I am indebted for this and for subsequent distinctions of a similar nature in this chapter to Claude Lévi-Strauss, 'The Structural Study of Myth', *Structural Anthropology* (New York and London: Basic Books, 1963) p. 224; and Edmund Leach, 'Genesis as Myth', *Genesis as Myth and Other Essays* (London: Cape, 1969) pp. 1–35.

6. See, especially, Samuel Holt Monk, 'The Pride of Lemuel Gulliver', *SR*, LXIII (1955) 48–71.

7. W. B. Carnochan, *Lemuel Gulliver's Mirror for Man* (Berkeley and Los Angeles: University of California Press, 1968) p. 11.

8. In this view, Swift's version of Gulliver's fall is as different from the orthodox doctrine as his conception of the 'natural Pravity' of the Yahoos is from the orthodox doctrine of original sin. When John Wesley cites the Yahoos as emblems of original sin, he is following, not the actual text, but his own spiritualized interpretation of it (Wesley's references are cited by T. O. Wedel, *Studies in Philology*, XXIII [1926], p. 442).

9. William H. McNeill, *The Pursuit of Power*, p. 160.

10. The most succinct survey of this tradition can be found in Dustin H. Griffin, *Satires against Man: the Poems of Rochester* (Berkeley, [etc.]: University of California Press, 1973) pp. 156–82. See also James E. Gill, 'Beast over Man: Theriophiliac Paradox in Gulliver's "Voyage to the Country of the Houyhnhnms"', *SP*, LXVII (1970) 532–49.

11. R. S. Crane, 'The Houyhnhnms, the Yahoos, and the History of Ideas', in *Reason and the Imagination: Studies in the History of Ideas, 1600–1800*, ed. J. A. Mazzeo (New York and London: Columbia University Press, 1962) pp. 231–53.

12. This point was noticed, though with different conclusions, by Hugo M. Reichard, 'Gulliver the Pretender', *PLL*, I (1965) 325–6.

13. Claude Lévi-Strauss, 'The Scope of Anthropology', in *Structural Anthropology, Volume II* (Chicago: University of Chicago Press, 1976) pp. 28–9.

14. Claude Lévi-Strauss, *The Raw and the Cooked: Introduction to a Science of Mythology*, I (New York and Evanston: Harper & Row, 1969) pp. 140–3, 176. See also, 'The Culinary Triangle', *New Society*, no. 221 (22 Dec. 1966) 937–40.

15. For related but distinct defenses of the Houyhnhnms, see William H. Halewood, 'Plutarch in Houyhnhnmland', *PQ*, XLIV (1965) 185–94; John F. Reichert, 'Plato, Swift and the Houyhnhnms', *PQ*, XLVII (1968) 179–92; and Eugene R. Hammond, 'Nature–Reason–Justice in *Utopia* and *Gulliver's Travels*', *SEL*, XXII (1982) 445–68.

CHAPTER 6: 'NOT IN TIMON'S MANNER'

1. This uncertainty is reflected in the polarization of critical opinion on the issue. For the view that Gulliver's misanthropy stems from his idealism, see, e.g. George Sherbern, 'Errors Concerning the Houyhnhnms', *MP*, 56 (1958) 92–7; and R. S. Crane, 'The Houyhnhnms, the Yahoos and the History of Ideas', op. cit., pp. 231–53. The conviction that Gulliver is a victim of pride is represented, for example, by John F. Ross, 'The Final Comedy of Lemuel Gulliver', *Studies in the Comic, University of California Publications in English*, 8 (1941) pp. 192–3; and Samuel H. Monk, 'The Pride of Lemuel Gulliver', *Sewanee Review*, 63 (1955) pp. 51–2.

2. *The Correspondence of Jonathan Swift*, ed. Harold Williams, 4 vols. (Oxford: Clarendon Press, 1963) III, 103. All citations to Swift's letter to Pope are to this edition.

3. Crane, 'The Houyhnhnms, the Yahoos, and the History of Ideas', pp. 248–9.

4. Aristotle's *Topics*, II, v; V, iv; I, v, in *Porphyrii Isagogem et Aristotle's Organum. Commentarius analyticis* [Auctore] Julius Pacius, 1597; rpt. (Hildesheim: George Olm, 1967) pp. 592, 670, 669. T. O. Wedel emphasized the Stoic origins of the definition *'animal rationale'* ('On the Philosophical Background of *Gulliver's Travels*', pp. 443–5).

5. Monk has drawn attention to the importance of the distinction between individuals and groups in Swift's letter ('The Pride of Lemuel Gulliver', pp. 51–2).

6. The first commentators to discuss the significance of Captain Mendez as an exemplary figure and foil to Gulliver were probably John F. Ross, 'The Final Comedy of Lemuel Gulliver', pp. 192–3; and Arthur E. Case, *Four Essays on Gulliver's Travels* (Princeton University Press, 1945) pp. 120–1.

7. For a different interpretation of Gulliver's clothing, see Max Byrd, 'Gulliver's Clothes: An Enlightenment Motif', *EnE*, 3 (1972) 41–6.

8. *Gulliver and the Gentle Reader: Studies in Swift and Our Time* (London and Boston: Routledge & Kegan Paul, 1973) p. 27.
9. Quoted from Margaret T. Hodgen, *Early Anthropology in the 16th and 17th Centuries* (Philadelphia: University of Pennsylvania Press, 1964) p. 367. Hodgen's chapter, 'The Problem of Savagery', pp. 354–85, is a thorough treatment of this tradition in Western European thought of the period.

Index

absolutism, 26–30
'Account of the Court and Empire
  of Japan', 26–7
Alexander, Jean, 103n
anthropology, ix, 2, 3
*Argument Against Abolishing
  Christianity*, 99
Aristotle: *Topics*, 94, 110n

Baudelaire, Charles, 103n
Boyle, John, fifth Earl of Orrery,
  103n
Brown, Norman O., 74, 103n
Burnet, Thomas, 106n
Byrd, Max, 110n

Carnochan, W. B., 80
Case Arthur E., 110n
Chardin, Jean: *Travels in Persia*, 8,
  105n, 106n
Cooke, Edward: *A Voyage to the
  South Sea and Around the
  World*, 8, 104n
Cotton, Charles, 106n
'country ideology', 22, 23, 39, 43,
  61, 65–6, 95
Crane, R. S., 84, 94, 109n, 110n

Dampier, William: *A New Voyage
  Around the World*, 8, 104n
Defoe, Daniel: *Robinson Crusoe*, 8,
  104n; *Captain Singleton*, 109n
'Description of the Morning',
  16–17
Deuteronomy, 105n
Dickinson, H. T., 39, 105n, 107n
dirt, 15–17; its linkage to dust, 67
Douglas, Mary, xi, 1–2, 9, 20, 103n
Downie, J. A., 105n

Ehrenpreis, Irvin, 47, 107n
England in the Age of Walpole,
  27, 38–9

*Enquiry into the Behavior of the
  Queen's Last Ministry*, 49, 107n

Fabricant, Carole, 106n
Fink, Z. S., 107n
Frantz, R. W., 104n, 109n
Frye, Roland M., 74, 109n
Fussell, Paul, Jr., 104n

Gay, John, 74
Geertz, Clifford, 108n
Gennep, Arnold van, 9, 104n
Gilbert, William, 55
Gill, James E., 109n
Greene, Donald, 60, 108n
Griffith, Dustin, 109n
Gulliver, Lemuel: role in narrative,
  7, 9; process of adaptation to
  exotic cultures, 11–14; source
  of contagion in Lilliput, 18–21;
  disgust in Brobdingnag, 31–5;
  duplicity as patriot hero in
  Brobdingnag, 42, 51–2; initial
  response to Yahoos, 73–5;
  interiorization of loathing, 79;
  alteration in response to
  Yahoos, 80; return from
  Houyhnhnmland, 93; satirist
  in England, 99–100
Gulliver's Travels: nature of its
  societies, 3–8; their differing
  norms of purity, 2, 14–16;
  structural pattern of the four
  Voyages, 8–11
  Part I: Lilliputian system of
  classification, 4; its rivalry
  with Blesfescu, 4, 28–9; its
  pollution rules, 19–21;
  Lilliput as theater state, 4,
  24, 26; its original
  constitution, 21–3;
  Lilliputian despotism, 24,
  26–30; Flimnap and Skyresh

112